BROKERED
BETRAYALS

AIMEE NICOLE WALKER

BROKERED
BETRAYALS

CHAPTER ONE

ROYCE PARKED THE SUV AND TURNED SOLEMN EYES TO HIS husband, or so he hoped that was the message he conveyed. When Sawyer only snorted, he decided not to quit his day job to pursue a career in acting. "After tonight, I never want you to doubt my love for you."

Sawyer rolled his eyes hard enough to sprain something. "I have never doubted your love for me, and if I did, your piss-poor commitment to consuming cauliflower crust pizza for a single night wouldn't change my mind."

Royce gasped and aimed for an expression of shock and outrage.

Sawyer bit his lip to keep from chuckling, but his body vibrated with repressed laughter until it burst free. "You look constipated, which makes me wonder if we should've chosen vegan cheese for the pizza. Dairy can be a binder and a bloater."

"I... You..." The mere suggestion was enough to make Royce stammer. "Just no," he finally said. "That's a crime against humanity that I will not abide." Sawyer consumed more than his fair share of cheese, so Royce suspected—desperately hoped—he was pulling his leg.

"It's a choice, not a crime," Sawyer said.

"Okay, then I *choose* real cheese."

Sawyer arched a brow. "And I'd like the record to show that I offered to order a meat lover's pizza for you."

"Let the record show? Are you addressing a courtroom?" Royce asked.

"Well, I have a law degree from—"

"Duke University," Royce interjected with a voice as hoity-toity as he could make it.

"Yes," Sawyer said. "But the record I referred to was our marital one."

Sensing they were about to engage in their favorite game of Who Does It Best, Royce unclipped his seat belt and turned toward Sawyer as much as the middle console allowed. They'd turned bantering about random topics into a sexy art form where they'd take their debate to the sheets instead of the streets. By the time they finished, neither of them would remember what subject they'd been debating. Royce mentally rubbed his hands together as he cocked a brow. "Who's keeping score, and what kind of point system are we using?"

Sawyer's dark eyes turned ornery as he notched his chin higher, ready to take on the challenge. "There have been plenty of times when one of us sacrifices his wants and needs to make the other happy."

"It's called compromising," Royce volleyed. "That's what married people do. Let the record show that I'm being the mature adult right now."

"See!" Sawyer cried. "Don't pretend you don't tally things up in your head so you can remind me later if I complain about my sacrifice."

"Give me an example." When Sawyer gestured to the pizza, Royce waved him off. "Besides that."

"Okay, then I use every other meal as my exhibits. You frequently put on a brave face and regret it later. Remember the sushi fiasco?"

Royce shivered hard. "I wanted to try it," he lied.

Sawyer cocked his head to the side and narrowed his eyes. "You bargained sexual favors before agreeing to try it and then went to Taco Bell afterward."

"I seem to recall someone in this vehicle had ordered a Chalupa and a steak quesadilla," Royce replied. "Not saying who, but if I did, the name would start with an S and rhyme with lawyer." They both snickered at their ridiculous mock argument. "So, if I'm sacrificing for food, what are you giving up?"

"Movies, shows, music, vacation spots, and—"

"Yeah, okay," Royce said. "I get it. I'm a pain in the ass."

Sawyer smiled devilishly and waggled his eyebrows. "Don't threaten me with a good time."

"Hey! That's my line," Royce said. "Let's toss these pizza boxes on Eddie and Jo's new porch and run."

Sawyer took off his seat belt and leaned toward him. "You know we can't do that. Eddie spent an entire day helping you build Darla's nursery furniture, and Jo helped me wash and fold all her pretty outfits. Helping them settle into their new place is the least we can do. And I've never seen your dad this happy."

"You're right." With a dramatic sigh, Royce turned off the engine and opened his door. "But we're picking up where we left off when we get home."

"I'll be disappointed if we don't," Sawyer replied.

The sun had set, and the temperature hovered just below fifty degrees. Royce zipped his jacket higher to ward against the chill. The weather had been overcast and gloomy all day, reminding Royce how much he usually disliked winter. But this year was different because January marked the last stretch until their baby girl arrived. No cold snap or cloudy days could ruin his excitement. Not even cardboard… er…cauliflower crust pizza.

Leaning closer to Sawyer, he said, "So, which of us is on top right now?"

Sawyer stopped on the front porch and turned to face Royce instead of ringing the doorbell. Stepping closer until only the pizza boxes separated them, Sawyer said, "I might have the upper hand right now, but we both know you'll end up on top by the end of the night."

The door swung open before Royce could jerk the pizza boxes from Sawyer's hands and throw them on the porch. "Do you guys need a few minutes?" Jo asked.

"Yes," Royce replied at the same time Sawyer said, "No."

Jo giggled. "Well, come inside when you're ready." She walked away, leaving them alone on the porch. When Eddie asked what was going on, she said, "The happy husbands are having a moment."

Her remark drew Eddie to the door, but Royce and Sawyer kept their eyes on one another. "Is this guy giving you trouble?"

Royce forced his gaze away from Sawyer just long enough to catch his dad's thumb hooked in his direction. "Every damn chance I get," he responded as he got lost in warm brown eyes once again.

Sawyer's full mouth curved into a sexy smirk. "And twice on Sundays."

"Would've been thrice in my younger days," Royce replied with an unmistakable leer.

Eddie's snort interrupted their playful banter. "You guys can just hand over the pizza and go home if there's something else you'd rather be doing. Jo and I took some personal time off from work to unpack and make this place a home. It doesn't all need to be done tonight."

Royce forced himself to meet Eddie's impish gaze. "And miss your reaction to tasting that pizza?" He shook his head. "Hell no. Besides, we want to see the new place. Surely there's something we can help you with."

"You can help him hang up his television," Jo called from inside the house. "He's putting on a brave front about not watching ESPN tonight, but I know better."

Eddie laughed as he stepped aside to let them in. "Busted. Guess there are a few things I'd like to tackle before bed."

"We could've helped you more if you'd moved over the weekend like most people do instead of doing this on a Tuesday," Royce said. "Or at least given us some notice so we could've taken time off from work."

"We saved a lot of money doing it this way. I have a mortgage now and need to watch my pennies." Eddie beamed with pride at being a first-time homeowner. "And besides, you're having a baby soon. You need to save all your personal time off to be with your little girl."

"That's thoughtful of you, Eddie," Royce said, "but you have two other adult children and healthy teenage grandsons who could've helped out. This was a big undertaking."

"I'm fitter than I've been in years." Eddie flexed his arm to prove the point. He had lost weight and put on more muscle, resembling the man he used to be twenty years ago. Thank fuck his attitude hadn't reverted back to that time too. "I have more energy than I know what to do with on most days." Eddie looked around the room and added, "Besides, the moving guys did the heavy lifting. I just need to hang the televisions."

"And assemble the bed," Jo suggested.

"Right." Eddie waggled his brows at his son.

Sawyer snickered and steered the conversation in a safer direction. "This place looks so much bigger on the inside."

"It reminds me of your house," Eddie said. "The open floor plan makes you feel connected even when you're not in the same room."

The living room was already set up except for the television and a scattering of boxes. Instead of buying new furniture, Eddie and Jo brought their favorite pieces from their homes and donated the rest. The hyper-masculine and ultra-feminine styles should've clashed horribly, but they formed a beautiful and unique union instead, much like Eddie and Jo.

"You guys have been here for less than a day, and the place feels like a home already," Royce said.

Eddie looked around as he scratched the back of his neck. "You like it?"

"It's a beautiful representation of both of you," Sawyer said.

Eddie puffed up a little at the compliment. "Wait until Jo hangs up her artwork. She has more talent in her little toe than I have in my entire body."

Royce patted Eddie's back. "I married up, so I know what you mean."

Sawyer rolled his eyes and lifted the pizza boxes higher. "Is anyone hungry?"

"Come on into the kitchen," Jo called out. "I just need to find the box with the plates."

"We can use paper towels," Eddie said.

"Okay. I need to find which box I put them in."

"Don't bother on my account," Royce told her. "I'd be more than happy to just eat my pizza while standing over the box."

"Of course you would," Sawyer said.

Eddie chuckled and shook his head. "Neanderthal."

They all pitched in and searched the boxes until they located the paper towels. Royce tamped down his enthusiasm for the pizza, knowing they would likely have a seventy-thirty ratio in favor of vegetable toppings, but his hopes rose when the pizza box lids went up. The crust was thin and crispy, and the cheese was a golden brown that screamed it had come from a cow and not… He didn't know where vegan cheese came from and decided not to give it another thought. Who cared if the pizza was loaded down with caramelized vegetables and drizzled with a brown liquid when it smelled like pure heaven? The second pizza offered circles of mozzarella and basil leaves.

Jo clapped her hands and took a big slice of the first pizza. "The happy hippie," she said reverently.

"What's the brown stuff?" Eddie asked.

"A balsamic reduction," Sawyer said. "It's so good."

Royce picked up a slice and studied it closely. "I'll be the judge of that."

"And I'll wait while you do," Eddie quipped.

Jo had a mouthful of pizza, so she nudged Eddie with her elbow.

"Some changes have been harder to make," Eddie admitted. "I prefer at least three different meats on my pizza and maybe a smattering of mushrooms."

"Amen." Royce saluted his father with his pizza slice and then took a tentative bite. The explosion of flavors on his tongue made his taste buds sing, and the combination of textures was surprisingly pleasing. Royce wanted to string Eddie along and irritate Sawyer by pretending the pizza was barely passable, but he ruined his efforts by going in for a second bite too quickly.

"Good enough for me," Eddie said as he grabbed a slice of the veggie pizza.

Sawyer looked smug as hell when he bit through mozzarella and basil.

"This pizza joint makes the best cauliflower crust," Jo said.

Eddie held the slice closer to his face and scrutinized it as he chewed. "Cauliflower? Never mind. It tastes great." Then he shrugged and went in for a second bite.

They devoured the happy hippie and turned desperate eyes to the Margherita pizza that remained.

"Basil and mozzarella, huh?" Eddie asked.

Sawyer laughed. "And tomatoes."

Eddie shrugged and went for it. His face formed a "not bad" expression as he chewed.

Jo passed out drinks, and they chatted about random things until they finished eating. Sawyer stayed in the kitchen to help Jo unpack, and Royce followed Eddie to their bedroom suite to set up the bed and mount the television there too. They worked in companionable silence for a while, only talking when they needed the other to hand them a tool or provide support. Royce sensed Eddie had something on his mind, and a quick glance revealed a slight furrow in his dad's brow.

"What's weighing on you, Eddie?"

His dad looked up, and the furrow deepened. "Nothing. I was just concentrating on making sure the bed is level."

Royce set the drill on the nightstand and gave Eddie his full attention. "Nah. You've seemed distracted the last few times I've seen you. It feels like you have something you want to say but are worried that maybe you shouldn't."

Eddie dropped his gaze for a few moments before meeting Royce's eyes again. "Yeah, maybe I do. Things are great between us." Eddie swallowed hard. "The best they've ever been."

Royce nodded. "And you think whatever you have to say or ask will make me mad enough to stop speaking to you again?"

Eddie seemingly held his breath for a few seconds before he released it. "Yes. That's what I'm worried about."

It irritated Royce that Eddie had deemed him too sensitive or irrational to hear his thoughts without getting offended. Then he realized this was the exact reaction his dad had wanted to avoid. He could already feel his body temperature rising and his pulse increasing. Royce took a deep breath and sighed. "It's not much of a relationship if we can't speak our minds."

"True, but you've taught me that some things are better left unsaid."

"Unless it's causing you undue stress," Royce told him. His mind spun with all the potential sources of trouble, but Royce's thoughts kept returning to his two vulnerable spots: Sawyer and Darla. But Eddie was crazy about Sawyer, and he was excited to meet his first granddaughter. Royce took another one of those cleansing breaths Sawyer was so fond of and allowed his dad to say what was on his mind without automatically leaping to worst conclusions. They both deserved better.

A chuckle rumbled in Eddie's chest as he shook his head. "I can hear your wheels turning, son. I'm not thinking bad thoughts about your man or disapproving of the situation with your baby girl."

"I know." Or he was mostly sure. "What is going on?"

"I've just been wondering about how the adoption will work," Eddie said. "You guys haven't discussed it much."

"Because it's not a simple process," Royce replied.

Eddie nodded. "I figured as much, and I didn't want to be nosy or bring up sensitive subjects."

"I'm sure most people are curious. I just figured they cared more about the outcome than the process."

"But I'm your dad, and I do care," Eddie said. "What makes your adoption so difficult? Is it because you're a same-sex couple?" Eddie's tone had turned gruff, and he crossed his arms over his chest as if ready to go to battle on a moment's notice.

"Not in this case," Royce said. "Our complication has to do with the type of surrogacy we've chosen."

Eddie cocked his head to the side. "There's more than one?"

Royce chuckled, then leaned against the dresser. "There are two: gestational and traditional. The gestational surrogate is not the baby's biological mother, where a traditional surrogate is. The gestational surrogate is the preferred method, but Sawyer and I didn't want to go that route. We love that Kelsey is Darla's biological mother, even if that causes us additional legal hurdles."

"How so?"

"Our adoption process can't start until after Darla arrives," Royce explained. "If Kelsey wasn't her mother, we'd be able to arrange a pre-birth order so that both my and Sawyer's names would appear on the birth certificate from the jump. We'd have the legal documents ahead of time, granting us custody and the rights to make decisions about Darla's medical care."

"But you're her biological father. Doesn't that count?"

"I am, and no one is contesting that, but mothers are considered the primary parent," Royce explained. "The hospital won't release Darla into my custody without a court order."

"Jesus," Eddie said. "Does that mean Darla has to live with Kelsey until the adoption goes through?"

"No. We hired a legal team to guide us through the process before our first visit to the fertility clinic. We signed a surrogacy agreement up front, and we've known all along what to expect."

Eddie's big, meaty paw landed on Royce's shoulder and squeezed. "Doesn't make it any easier though, does it?"

"Not at all."

"So, what has to happen before Darla can come home with her dads?" Eddie asked.

"The three of us are meeting with our legal teams to finalize the documentation tomorrow evening. I had to prove my paternity, which wasn't hard since we used a clinic, and Kelsey will sign a document to waive her parental rights. Once Darla is born, the documentation goes to a judge, who will then grant temporary custody to me so I can bring her home."

"When does Sawyer get to become her daddy too?" Eddie asked. "Legally, I mean."

"We'll have to complete a home study and—"

"Home study?" Eddie bellowed. "What kind of homophobic shit is that?"

Royce patted his broad shoulder. "Take it easy, killer. Home studies are required for all adoptions, not just those involving same-sex parents. The court will also require physicals, background checks, and character reference letters." Royce could tell by Eddie's scowl that he was getting worked up. "Everyone has to do this with adoptions.

We could face homophobia with the person completing the home study or with the judge who signs off on the post-birth order or approves the second-parent adoption later, but I can't let my mind go there."

Eddie released a little growl. "How does the second-parent thing work?"

"Once we complete the steps I mentioned, the paperwork goes to family court, and they'll set a finalization date where we go before a judge to get the adoption approved. A new birth certificate will be ordered that names Sawyer and me as Darla's parents. It shouldn't take long for everything to process because we've already done most of the legwork. We've completed our background checks and physicals and gathered enough reference letters to paper the courthouse."

Eddie's brow furrowed slightly, and hurt registered in his gray eyes before he blinked it away. "You didn't ask me to write a letter. Is it because I'm a felon?"

"Of course not."

"You don't trust me to write a letter?" Eddie asked, his voice ticking up a notch as if offended.

"No," Royce replied. "We didn't ask any of our family members to write letters for us."

"What? Why?"

"Because family members aren't objective," Royce explained. "We chose colleagues and friends."

"Don't you think the judge will find it weird?"

"Our lawyers don't think so, but write a character reference if you'd like. I'll happily submit it to our legal team."

Eddie rubbed the back of his neck. "I don't know. I'm not as smart as Barron. He's a respectable member of the community and would make a better reference."

"You're my dad," Royce said. "You're an amazing grandfather. Little Darla is going to be so lucky to have you in her life."

Eddie pulled Royce into a fierce hug and held on longer than usual. "You're the best part of me, kid. Never doubt that."

"I won't." Royce pulled back from the embrace and smiled at his dad. "I won't forget to tell Jace and Dru that you said it either."

"Shithead," Eddie snarled as he playfully reached for him.

Royce danced out of the way, bobbing and weaving until he bumped into the bed frame they'd been building. Eddie had him cornered, but Royce wasn't afraid of his dad like he'd been as a kid. Laughter and orneriness sparkled in Eddie's gray eyes instead of rage and misery. Royce held his hands up in mock surrender anyway. It was getting late, and he was eager to get his husband home. "We have our marching orders, and we best get to them."

Eddie snorted and changed direction to the other side of the bed, where he hoisted that side of the headboard into the slot. "Bring me the drill?"

Royce grabbed it from the nightstand and carried it to Eddie, who screwed the headboard to the frame. Eddie gave the bed a good shake. "Nice and sturdy. Good." He shot a wink at Royce, probably hoping to make him uncomfortable.

"I'll do you one better," Royce said. He withdrew a twelve-inch level from Eddie's toolbox and placed it in the center of the headboard. The bubble landed dead center, and Royce stood back with a nod. "Good to go."

They unrolled the wooden slats, positioned them in the bottom of the bed frame, and screwed them to the rail. Then came the bulky mattress. They wrestled the heavy son of a bitch into place and sat down to catch their breath.

"Whew!" Eddie exclaimed. "I talked a big game earlier, but I'm not getting any younger."

"But thankfully, you are getting older," Royce countered.

Eddie pointed at him and winked. "Good thinking." He grabbed the linens from a box and set them on the bed. "Jo and I can handle this part."

"Why wait?" Royce picked up the fitted sheet and shook it out. "Let's do this."

Eddie got quiet again as they worked, and Royce could tell he wanted to ask more questions.

"Just ask, Eddie. I won't get mad."

"Does it worry you that Kelsey might change her mind?" Eddie held up his hands before Royce could reply. "I didn't mean it to sound like that, but it must be difficult for her. I'd think it would be next to impossible for Kelsey not to form a bond with a baby growing inside her, even if the child wasn't her biological daughter."

"Sometimes it is hard for her," Royce said. "She's been very honest about it. And we're grateful for the bond she feels for Darla because we've chosen Kelsey and Andrew as her godparents. Darla will always know that Kelsey's act of love brought her into the world."

"She's an amazing woman to give you this gift," Eddie said.

"One of the fiercest, most loving women I know."

"Does she get compensated?" Eddie asked.

"Kelsey won't let us pay for anything except her medical care, so we established a college fund for Ella with the surrogate fee she waived," Royce replied. "Our agreement also covers paying for any emotional support she'll need after Darla's delivery and filling any salary gaps not covered by her maternity leave and supplemental insurance."

Eddie ran a hand over his scruffy jaw. "Sounds expensive."

"But worth every dime." Royce placed the last decorative pillow on the bed and stepped back to survey their handiwork. "Not bad." He leaned forward and gave them a chop in the center. "Better." Royce turned to his dad. "Is there anything else you want to ask? Nothing's off-limits."

Eddie raked his teeth over his bottom lip. "Why'd you choose the name Darla? I figured you'd name your little girl after your mama."

"Jace called dibs on Mom's name when Holly was pregnant with Harper. They plan to have more kids, so the dibs are still in effect in case they have a girl."

Eddie chuckled. "Is that a written rule or something you guys made up?"

"Honor among brothers," Royce replied. "And naming our little girl Darla just feels right to me."

"You always shared a special bond with your Aunt Tipsy. She was a hell of a woman who always did the right thing."

Royce cocked his head to the side. "I thought the two of you hated one another."

"Hate's a strong word." Eddie placed both hands on his lower back and stretched his spine. "It's true she hated the things I did, but I don't think Darla ever fully gave up on me. And I respected the hell out of her when she stepped up for you kids after I went to prison. Did you know she wrote me letters while I was locked up?"

Royce's eyebrows disappeared into his hairline. "No. She never told us that."

Eddie nodded. "She didn't write every week, but close to it."

"Why?"

"She kept me updated on what was going on with you kids, and sometimes she included photographs. Watching you guys grow up without me was hard as hell." Eddie swallowed hard and averted his eyes for a few moments before meeting Royce's gaze again. "It was especially hard when you refused to live with me after my release." He held up his hand before Royce could respond. "I understood why, but I still hated it. You made the correct choice then, and you've continued to make the best decisions for yourself ever since." Eddie's eyes misted over, and he rubbed the moisture away with a knuckle. "Anyway, I found the stash of letters from Tipsy when I packed up my place to move. Do you want them?"

Royce was incredibly moved that Eddie had kept them. "Of course. Thank you."

"I'll bring them over after I figure out which one of the boxes they're in."

"Appreciate it."

Eddie's eyes got suspiciously moist again when he hooked an arm around Royce's neck and pulled him in. "I'm turning into a big, old softy."

"Bet your lady likes it."

"Sure does," Eddie said. "I'm a very lucky man."

"That you are. You have a beautiful new home to share with a wonderful woman."

"I can't wait to show you the backyard. It's too dark to get the full effect, but it's the perfect spot for family barbecues or an intimate wedding."

Royce cocked a brow. "Are you trying to tell me something?"

Eddie worried his bottom lip between his teeth and looked behind him to make sure no one was standing outside the bedroom. "I'm going to ask Jo to marry me," he whispered.

Royce grinned like an idiot at his father. "That's the best news. When?"

"I haven't worked out the details yet," Eddie replied. "But soon."

"Don't wait too long, or you'll talk yourself out of it." Sawyer's and Jo's combined laughter carried down the hallway and made Royce smile. "That woman is crazy about you, and you deserve this happiness."

"Thank you, son. That means so much coming from you." Eddie wiped his eyes with the back of his hand and cleared his throat. "Now, let's hang these televisions up so you fellas can be on your way. I'm sure you have things you'd rather do."

Royce chuckled. "Sounds to me like you're trying to get rid of us so you can have Jo all to yourself."

Winking, Eddie said, "You're not wrong."

Royce picked up the drill, flexed his bicep, and pulled the trigger a few times to make it whir. "Get out your gun show, Eddie, and let's make our favorite people swoon."

CHAPTER TWO

SAWYER GREETED KELSEY WITH A WARM HUG WHEN SHE exited her car. He and Royce had bundled up like it was twenty below, while Kelsey just wore an ivory cardigan over her cheetah-print turtleneck and black corduroy overalls. "Aren't you freezing?" Sawyer asked when she stepped back from their embrace.

Kelsey giggled as she rubbed her hand over her baby bump. "I'm putting off enough heat for three people," she told him. "Trust me. I'm not cold, but I have winter gear in the car in case of an emergency." Kelsey opened her arms and hugged Royce next. "Miguel called and said he's running a few minutes behind. He said we should go inside and get comfortable. He'll be here before we know it."

Miguel Perez was the lawyer Kelsey had chosen to represent her throughout the surrogate process. He was a snazzy dresser and more handsome than one man had the right to be, but he was perpetually running behind schedule. Sawyer didn't get the impression his tardiness was because of arrogance, but it still annoyed him. They had four weeks left until Darla's due date, and it was crunch time. All their legal planning appointments were important, but this one was the most significant because Kelsey would relinquish her parental rights to Darla so that Royce and Sawyer could bring her home from the hospital. It was a temporary agreement until their adoption became permanent, but it was the first big step to making it happen. Sawyer hadn't wanted to wait so long, but their attorneys assured them it was a standard practice with traditional surrogates since the paperwork couldn't go before a judge until after Darla was born. Still, the last-minute stuff created a knot of tension in his chest that made it hard for him to breathe.

Sawyer took Kelsey's hand as they headed toward Owens, McKinley, and Reese Family Law. "How are you feeling?"

They both knew it was a loaded question, but Kelsey met his gaze with a smile. "I'm feeling great today."

A car stopped in the parking lot near them, and Sawyer glanced over out of caution. Andrew exited the rear seat and thanked the driver before shutting the door and jogging to them.

Kelsey released Sawyer's hand and met her husband halfway. Andrew wrapped his brawny arms around her, then rubbed his hands up and down her back.

"Where's your coat?" Andrew asked.

"See," Sawyer said. "It's freezing."

Kelsey scowled at him over her shoulder. "It's forty-five degrees. People up north would kill for temperatures like this in January." She turned back around to smile at her husband. "I didn't know you were coming. I would've picked you up."

"Last-minute decision." Cupping her face, Andrew brushed his thumb over her cheek. "Ella is with my mom, and I thought we could enjoy a nice dinner after your appointment. I ordered a ride and left my car at the office. We can swing by and get it later tonight, or you can drop me off on your way to work in the morning."

Kelsey leaned into his touch and sighed. "You're the best."

Royce linked his fingers with Sawyer's and led him away to give the couple some privacy, humming Tina Turner's "Simply the Best" as they went.

"Yes, you are," Sawyer said. He glanced over his shoulder and saw that Kelsey and Andrew were still in the same spot. Kels had rested her head on Andrew's shoulder, and he rocked her from side to side as if dancing in place. She wore an expression of pure bliss, not sorrow or regret, and the knot in Sawyer's chest eased slightly.

"After you," Royce said, recapturing Sawyer's attention. He'd opened the large mahogany door and gestured for Sawyer to enter ahead of him.

Sawyer stopped long enough to kiss his cheek before stepping inside the warm building. Their law firm was on the second floor, so they took the stairs and entered the waiting room. The receptionist looked up from her task and greeted them with a smile.

"Hi, guys," Lola said. "Will it just be the two of you meeting with Ivy this evening?"

"No," Sawyer replied. "Kelsey and her husband will be up in a few minutes. Mr. Perez will also be here, though he's running a little behind."

"No problem. I'll just let Ivy know you're here, and I'll set you up in the conference room."

Sawyer walked over to the fancy hot beverage bar while Lola spoke quietly into her phone. "Do you want something?"

"No, thanks," Royce replied.

Sawyer prepared a fancy hot chocolate with an abundance of marshmallows for Kelsey and a salted caramel coffee for himself.

"You're a rock star," Kelsey said when Sawyer handed the steaming cup to her.

"Do you want anything, Andrew?" Sawyer asked. They'd stopped calling him Big Sexy after Alec left town, and it seemed like the big guy missed the endearment.

"Um, I'm not sure. Let me see what's available."

"Everything," Sawyer, Royce, and Kelsey said.

Andrew shook his head at the trio of trouble before heading over to the beverage bar.

"They have cold drinks in the minifridge below the counter, babe," Kelsey said.

Andrew grabbed an apple juice from the refrigerator and joined them.

Kelsey eyed the bottle as she sipped her hot chocolate. "That looks good too."

Her husband extended the juice to her with one hand and wiped the hot chocolate smudge off her lip with the other. "You can have it. I'll trade you."

Kelsey volleyed her gaze between the beverages as she tried to decide. Andrew chuckled and slid the juice into her handbag before retreating to grab another from the refrigerator.

Lola stood up and gestured for everyone to follow her to an elegantly appointed conference room. "Ivy is going to be with you in just a few minutes. I see you've grabbed something to drink already, but is there anything else I can get for you? We have some cookies in the break room."

"We're fine," Sawyer said. "Thank you."

Once Lola left, Royce leaned closer to him. "I could've really used a cookie." He sounded frazzled, and Sawyer turned to him in concern. The short drive from the precinct hadn't allowed much time for conversation, but Royce had seemed to be in a great mood.

"Rough day?"

"Nah," Royce replied. "I just like to rile you up."

Andrew flopped down into a chair and crossed his beefy arms over his chest like an overgrown toddler. "I wanted a cookie." The amount of petulance he injected into his voice made them laugh, and Sawyer's anxiety lessened even more. "I'm a big boy now. I can eat a cookie before dinner."

"And I'm a hundred months pregnant with your baby," Kelsey told Sawyer. "I wanted two cookies."

The relief Sawyer felt moments before dissipated, and his knot of tension tightened again. "I'm so sorry. I didn't mean to act as the group representative. Maybe I'm more nervous than I realized."

He liked to think he was in control of his own destiny, but this process reminded Sawyer that he was often just a passenger in his own damn life. But not a princess kind of passenger. He was more of a backseat driver. Royce's hand found his under the table and squeezed. Such a slight gesture shouldn't have a large impact on his mood, but it did. No matter what they faced, Sawyer wouldn't do it alone. He met Kelsey's soulful brown eyes, and her expression said, "I've got you." As he exhaled, Sawyer pictured his negative thoughts leaving his body along with his breath.

"I'll go ask Lola for some cookies," he said.

Kelsey reached across the table and took his hand. "Honey, I was just teasing. Sugar is the last thing I need right now. I had two cupcakes this afternoon."

Royce sat up straighter. "At work? Did someone bring in cupcakes?"

Shrugging, Kelsey said, "I think it was someone's birthday because there were dozens of cupcakes in the break room."

Royce looked at Sawyer with an outraged expression. "They forget about us basement dwellers at the precinct. No one thinks of calling downstairs to let us know there are sugary confections available."

Sawyer worked his bottom lip between his teeth. "Ummm."

Royce gasped as dramatically as a telenovela actress.

"Escandalosa," Kelsey declared as Andrew laughed.

"The betrayal," Royce agreed. "You knew there were cupcakes upstairs and didn't tell me." Royce narrowed his eyes and studied Sawyer's expression as he tried not to give in to the laughter building inside him. Then Royce leaned forward and sniffed Sawyer before widening his eyes. "You ate cupcakes without me?"

Sawyer slumped his shoulders and gave Royce his best sad puppy expression. He'd seen the gesture work for Dolly a hundred times. "I assumed you'd already ferreted out the sugar and carbs by the time I stumbled onto them," Sawyer replied. "And you were busy training the substitute instructors who are filling in for you during paternity leave."

Royce's brow shot up. He was not about to let this go. "You don't think Blue, Katie, and Diego would've enjoyed a cupcake?"

"That you have to train three people to fill your shoes says it all," Sawyer replied. "No time for cupcake breaks."

Kelsey gave the response a slow clap. "That's a Royce Locke level of bullshit right there."

Sawyer puffed out his chest and gave a mock bow. "Thank you. I have a dedicated instructor who is thorough and sexy as hell."

Narrowing his eyes, Royce said, "I'm not sure if I'm proud or disturbed. You didn't blink or even pause before you uttered such tripe. It just rolled off your tongue so easily."

"Imagine the habits he'll pick up from you after twelve weeks of paternity leave," Andrew said. "You'll barely leave the house for the first six weeks. So much togetherness."

Kelsey snorted and pointed across the table at Royce. "You think he'll stick out the full twelve weeks?"

"Hey!" Royce protested.

Kelsey shifted her finger to Sawyer. "And you think he'll allow it?"

"Hey!" Royce repeated.

Andrew and Kelsey locked gazes and conducted an entire silent conversation in a matter of seconds before bursting into laughter.

"I give it eight weeks before Royce climbs the walls," Andrew said.

Kelsey shook her head. "Nope, he'll paint them or tear them down in the name of renovation by the end of six weeks, and Sawyer will give him the boot."

Royce looked at Sawyer and shook his head. "I'd protest again, but they're not listening. At least you believe in me." When Sawyer didn't immediately respond, Royce gasped and clutched his chest. "Do you agree with them?"

"Idleness isn't in your wheelhouse. You're a doer, baby. I think the first six weeks will be easy to stay home because we'll be sleep deprived and getting used to new routines. But once we get a system down…"

"You think I'll get bored?" Royce asked.

"No, of course not. I think you'll just have excess energy if you're not getting enough activity."

Royce's brow furrowed into a dark scowl. "Like a dog?"

"He just keeps digging himself a deeper hole," Andrew told Kelsey. "Think we should bail your bestie out?"

Kelsey giggled. "If it helps, I sent Andrew back to work after a month. He was used to a fast-paced career, and it was a tough adjustment for him. He put his excess energy into 'helping' me, which sometimes felt a little..."

"Smothering," Andrew said. "And I kept hogging the remote control."

Laughing, Kelsey kissed his cheek. "That too. No offense, my love, but I'm happy that my mama is coming to help with Ella while I recover this time. She likes the same face-slapping dramas I do and wouldn't dream of turning on sports instead."

"No offense, my love, but I'm happy your mama is staying with us too. She's told me about the yummy food she plans to make for us while she's here."

Sawyer laughed at their antics, and the reverberation dislodged the tension balled in his chest. Sawyer exhaled slowly and looked around the conference room, taking in the framed accreditations and accolades on the walls interspersed with photos of the legal team posing with some of the families they'd assisted over the past two decades. They were in excellent hands and had nothing to worry about.

Royce's knee nudged his, pulling his attention back to him. "You good?"

Sawyer smiled. "I'm great."

Hushed voices from outside the conference room caught his attention. From his vantage point, Sawyer could see down the hallway to where Ivy spoke with a distinguished gentleman he recognized as the founding partner of the firm. At the moment, Ned Owens looked nothing like the smiling man in the photos on the wall. His posture was tense and his expression severe as he glanced at his watch.

"I was hoping to talk to you about a pressing matter before I left, but I don't want to keep your clients waiting," Ned said.

"Sorry," Ivy replied. "My phone call ran longer than I'd expected. I can make time now if you like. The clients are here, but Miguel is running behind."

Ned looked down the corridor and caught Sawyer watching their exchange. The older man didn't flinch, but he seemed very uncomfortable. He forced a smile and gave Sawyer a subtle nod before turning to Ivy. "That's okay. I'll call you later this evening." Ned checked his watch again. Was he really concerned about the time, or was he anxious about something else?

"Is everything okay?" Ivy asked.

"Of course," Ned replied, but nothing about his stiff posture or brisk tone offered assurances. "Ah, here comes Miguel now." The relief in his voice was palpable.

Ivy watched Ned closely as he shook hands with Miguel. She seemed unsettled by the entire encounter but snapped out of it when Miguel greeted her next.

Royce leaned into Sawyer's personal space and tried to peer down the hallway, but the angle wasn't right. "What caught your attention?"

"Miguel is here," Sawyer replied.

"Should I be jealous?"

"Would it stop you if he said no?" Kelsey teased.

Sawyer and Royce both laughed, then said, "No," at the same time.

"Ivy had a strange interaction with Ned Owens before Miguel arrived," Sawyer told them.

"Strange how?" Royce asked.

Kelsey leaned forward as far as her belly would allow. "Do tell."

"Nothing juicy," Sawyer replied. "Ned had wanted to talk to her about something before he left but didn't want to keep us waiting.

She told him that Miguel wasn't here yet and offered to make time for him then. Ned caught me watching them and declined, saying he'd call her later."

"That doesn't sound ominous," Andrew said, then furrowed his brow. "Unless you think he needed to talk to her about us."

Sawyer shook his head. "I didn't get that impression. He just seemed tense and checked his watch twice in thirty seconds."

"Anxious," Kelsey said, narrowing her eyes. "We've got ourselves a mystery, gang."

But Miguel and Ivy swept into the room before they could discuss the situation further. The group exchanged pleasantries with the attorneys as they sat at the table.

Ivy tucked a lock of straight black hair behind one ear and smiled at Kelsey. "How are you feeling?"

"I feel great, and Lil Sketti Squash is thriving."

"Not much longer now," Miguel said. He looked at Royce and Sawyer. "Are you guys ready?"

"Oh yeah," Royce said. "The nursery is ready, the car seats are assembled, and the hospital bags are packed."

Ivy opened a manila folder, and the sight of the paperwork made Sawyer's heart skip a beat. "I have Royce's proof of paternity and the post-birth order that establishes Royce and Sawyer Locke as the baby's intended parents."

Miguel opened a similar file and said, "And I have the post-birth relinquishment that Kelsey needs so Lil Sketti Squash can go home with her dads." The group laughed at his use of the nickname they'd given Darla at thirty-six weeks. She'd be their Lil Pumpkin before long. "Everyone should read the documents and ask questions before signing them."

Ivy passed her paperwork to Royce and Sawyer while Miguel did the same with Kelsey.

"You read it first since you speak legalese," Royce said.

It took staring at the page for a few seconds before Sawyer's brain allowed the letters to form words. He tried to maintain a sense of objectivity as he read the legal documents that would make their dreams a reality, but everything he'd learned in law school flew out the window. Sawyer's heart spiked, and he felt both hot and cold at the same time. Royce placed a calming hand on his knee, and Sawyer took steadying breaths until he focused on the words in front of him.

"Everything looks accurate to me," Kelsey said. "I'm ready to sign."

"I agree," Sawyer said as he slid the paperwork to Royce.

"I expected more documentation," Royce said.

"This is just the beginning," Ivy told him.

It didn't take Royce long to read through the paperwork. "I'm ready to sign too."

The attorneys had flagged the places that required their signatures, so the entire process was over in minutes.

"Great," Ivy said. "And now we wait until Lil Sketti Squash arrives. Call me as soon as she's born, day or night. I will send the post-birth order to the family court to get a judge's signature. That will trigger the rest of the tasks we need to complete before we can make the adoption official. Does anyone have questions?"

Sawyer and Royce looked at one another, then shook their heads.

"Kelsey?" Miguel asked.

"No, I'm good."

A few minutes later, the two couples were back outside. Sawyer held on to Kelsey longer than usual during their goodbye hug, but no one seemed to mind. Andrew and Royce chatted as they continued to their vehicles.

Kelsey pulled back and smiled at him. She'd traded in her heeled boots during the third trimester, but she was still nearly as tall as Sawyer in her flat boots. "Be honest. Did you worry I'd change my mind?"

"No," he replied. "I've never doubted you."

"I am going to miss this little girl, but I'd never hurt you guys that way," Kelsey told him.

"And we'll never keep her away from you," Sawyer replied. "She's always going to know that you're her biological mother." Sawyer squeezed her hand. "Have I ever told you how much I love you?"

"A time or two," Kelsey said with a smile. "And I love you too."

"Obviously." Sawyer kissed her cheek and led her toward the vehicles where their men waited. "Want to get pedicures on Saturday? I'll book the royal botanical treatments with all the extra bells and whistles."

"Yes, please."

"Enjoy dinner with your man," Sawyer said when they reached her car.

"Oh, I plan to, and I plan to enjoy it with your man too. Wednesday is half-price daiquiri nights at La Casita Bonita, including virgin ones. The first couple to the restaurant needs to grab a booth and order a gallon of queso cheese."

Sawyer chuckled as he opened the door for her. "Will do."

"And a virgin strawberry daiquiri for me," Kelsey said as she slid onto her seat.

"Got it."

Sawyer waited for her to swing her legs in and shut the door before getting in Royce's SUV.

"La Casita Bonita?" Royce asked.

"Is that okay with you?"

Royce snorted and backed out of his parking spot. "I've already planned my order." He glanced over at Sawyer with a smirk. "I'm going with low spice, and I'm skipping the beans because I have big plans for you later."

"This night keeps getting better."

Sawyer flipped off the bathroom light and strolled naked into their bedroom, anticipation propelling him forward, even though he wanted to pause and take in the sight of Royce stretched out on their bed and stroking himself. Desire had pulsed between them as they'd shared a delicious dinner, completed pet chores, and showered together. But it was more than expectation and excitement guiding Sawyer's feet that night or any. It was the delicious magnetic pull that Sawyer could never explain or cared to dissect. Royce was his North Star, and that's all he ever needed to know. And probably his husband's erect penis had something to do with his eagerness.

"I should've opened a bottle of the fancy wine you love so much," Royce said when Sawyer stopped by the side of the bed. "I think this occasion more than calls for it."

"Sex on a Wednesday night?"

Royce's hand stilled, and he rolled onto his side to face Sawyer. "Anytime I get you naked is a cause for celebration, but you know what I meant." He reached out and stroked his hand over Sawyer's thigh.

"I do." His words sounded as reverent as when Sawyer had spoken them at their wedding.

Royce's gray eyes became a tempest of emotion. "Still?"

Sawyer cupped his jaw and bent forward to kiss Royce's lips. "Always. No matter what life brings us."

Royce grabbed Sawyer's hips and pulled him onto the bed, rolling to pin him to the mattress. "This," Royce said, grinding his erection against Sawyer's. "We're going to have a lot of this." He reached into the headboard caddy and pulled out a small remote. He pressed a button, and LED candles flickered on around the room. A second remote turned off the overhead lights to create a romantic atmosphere.

Sawyer arched a brow. "What? No remote to turn on a sexy song?"

"Nope," Royce said with a wink. "Alexa, play 'Nice and Slow' by Usher."

The song played from a hidden speaker somewhere in the room. "This is new. When did you install bedroom speakers?"

"I set it up over the weekend and hid it until tonight." Royce lowered his head and kissed Sawyer's neck. "Do you want to ask more questions, or do you want to fuck?"

Sawyer gripped Royce's ass with both hands and thrust against him. "Nice and slow."

"You got it. Alexa, loop mode on."

"Loop mode on," came her robotic reply.

"Attagirl," Royce said.

They kissed and touched to the music's tempo, rolling their hips to the lazy rhythm as they joined their bodies together. Sawyer's breath hitched in his throat when Royce hovered above him and stared into his eyes, both of them knowing how the other felt. Sawyer cupped the back of Royce's neck and pulled him down for a kiss, and Royce moved inside him, nice and slow, building up his pleasure to the point of pain. Sawyer didn't need to ask for relief because Royce always knew what he needed. Hitching Sawyer's calves on his shoulders, Royce thrust deeper, finding the angle and pace that made him climax embarrassingly fast.

"Damn, you feel so good," Royce growled as he found his own release. He collapsed on top of him and tucked his head under Sawyer's chin.

"Playing 'Feel So Good' by Ashanti," Alexa said.

Royce growled in frustration this time, and Sawyer burst into laughter. "It's not funny."

"No," Sawyer agreed. "You've created a monster."

"Created a monster is usually a term that expresses regret or blame for unintentionally causing a negative outcome," Alexa informed them.

"Thank you, Alexa," Royce said.

"Playing 'thank u, next' by Ariana Grande," Alexa announced.

Royce spent the next few minutes trying to disable the device and ended up deactivating it. "We can't have her kicking off at random times and waking up the baby," Royce said as he flopped back down on the bed.

Sawyer rolled onto his side and rested his head on Royce's chest. "We're going to be dads."

Royce slid his hand into Sawyer's hair and massaged his scalp. "In a month or less."

"Could be longer," Sawyer said, though neither Kelsey nor they wanted that. "This pregnancy has felt like a time distortion. The first six months took forever, but the last two have passed in the blink of an eye."

"And I've loved sharing every second of it with you," Royce said.

"God, I can't wait to meet our daughter."

Royce swatted his ass. "Not much longer now. Let's hop back in the shower and clean off. We can watch a few episodes of *Animal Kingdom* before bed."

Sawyer didn't make it through one episode before he crashed into a deep sleep, only to be woken by a ringing phone. The digital numbers on his alarm clock said it was just after one in the morning, and he grabbed the phone off its charger before the call could go to voice-mail. The name on the caller ID made his heart stop.

"What's going on? Who's calling?" Royce asked groggily.

"It's Kelsey," Sawyer said, sounding way calmer than he felt. He accepted the call and put her on speaker. "Hey, Kels. What's up?"

"Your daughter must be very excited to meet her daddies because she's on her way."

"Right now?" Royce shrieked.

"Yep," Kelsey replied calmly. "I packed her off in a Lyft."

Royce scrubbed his eyes with his fists. "This is a dream, right?"

Sawyer tossed back the covers and got out of bed. "I don't think so."

Andrew's chuckle came through the connection. "Be nice. The guys are new to this."

"But I was having fun at their expense while I still have a sense of humor," Kelsey grumbled. "Things are about to get really painful for me."

"Kelsey," Andrew softly chided.

"Okay, fine. Lil Sketti Squash isn't in a Lyft heading your way, but my water broke. Ella is still with Andrew's mom, so we're just going to mosey on over to the hospital."

"We'll be right behind you." Sawyer calmly pulled clothes from the drawers for Royce and himself and tossed them on the bed. Darla's bags were packed and waiting in the hall by the garage door. They simply needed to get dressed and brush their teeth. He glanced at the bed, where Royce remained with a look of absolute shock on his face.

"Are you okay, Kels?" Sawyer asked. "Are you in pain?"

"Not yet," she replied cheerily. "But you'll be the first to know when that changes."

Sawyer laughed. He'd expected to be a ball of nerves when this call came, but a sense of calm and rightness had washed over him. "Drive carefully. Love you."

"Love you too," Kelsey said before disconnecting the call.

Sawyer tossed his phone onto the bed and reached for his jeans. Royce still hadn't moved by the time he'd pulled them on. Sawyer clapped his hands loudly and gave his best Cher impersonation when he said, "Snap out of it."

Royce blinked and looked around the room for a second before his gaze landed on Sawyer again. His eyes were as wide as saucers when he whispered, "We're having a baby."

"Yes, we are," Sawyer said as he tugged on his shirt.

"Today."

"Probably, though these things can take a while," Sawyer said. "Are you going to get dressed and go with me to meet our daughter, or are you going to stay here and wait for updates?"

Royce threw back the covers and bolted from the bed so fast that he stumbled and nearly fell. "Are we ready for this?"

It took everything Sawyer had not to laugh. "It's a little late to question it now."

Royce shook his head. "Not that. Do we have everything we need?"

"And then some," Sawyer said as he handed Royce his jeans. "And if we've overlooked something, we'll buy it."

"You're so calm right now." It almost sounded like an accusation.

"I know, right? I think it's a good look for me." Sawyer framed his face with his hands.

"And I'm freaking out," Royce said. "Why am I the one freaking out? It's like a weird role reversal. I don't think I like it."

"I'm kind of digging it," Sawyer said. "Do you need my help to get dressed?"

"What? No." Royce shook his head and seemed to snap out of it long enough to put on his clothes. But then he went to the closet and came back carrying a pair of flip-flops. "I'm ready."

Sawyer took the sandals from his hand and gave him a pair of socks. "Your shoes are by the garage door with all the baby stuff."

Royce sat down on the bed and pulled on a sock. "I don't think we packed enough stuff."

"We're taking enough for three babies."

"We're having three babies?" Royce asked. His pupils had dilated until only a tiny rim of his gray irises showed. Had he hit his head when he got out of bed?

"No, just one perfect baby girl."

"Are you sure?"

Sawyer bent down and put the second sock on Royce's foot before tugging him to an upright position. "We've had multiple ultrasounds, and I am confident we're only having one baby."

"Okay," Royce said.

The urge to run right out to the garage and fire up the car was strong, but Sawyer didn't want the hospital staff to think Royce was high. He sat his husband on an island stool while he filled a travel mug with strong coffee. "Drink your bean juice while I load the car."

"Okay."

But the travel mug sat in the same spot Sawyer had left it. "Ready?"

Royce bolted up from the stool. "Let's go." He dashed around the island and down the hall, stopping by the garage door to grab his keys off the hook.

Sawyer snatched them from his hands. "I don't think so."

"I'm fine to drive."

"You haven't blinked in ten minutes," Sawyer countered. "I'll drive." He tugged Royce close and kissed him hard. His husband blinked once, closed his eyelids, and returned the kiss. Sawyer pulled back after a few moments and stared into his husband's alert eyes. "There you are."

Royce blinked a couple of times, and a blush crept up his cheeks. "Where'd I go?"

"I don't know, and it doesn't matter. You're here now. Are you ready to meet our daughter?"

Laughter bubbled out of Royce. "God yes."

CHAPTER THREE

ROYCE WASN'T SURE IF HE WANTED TO LAUGH HYSTERICALLY or sob as Sawyer navigated the dark streets. It reminded him of the one time he'd performed with the middle school choir. He'd been trying to turn over a new leaf and be a better student. Royce had blown off the required participation in previous years and just didn't show up on performance night. Aunt Tipsy had encouraged him to try new things because Eddie wasn't around to ridicule his efforts. But having everyone's eyes on him during the performance made Royce so nervous that he forgot all the words and giggled uncontrollably for the duration of the set instead of bawling his eyes out. His music teacher, Mrs. Hildie, would've snatched him bald afterward if she'd been able to keep her job. She'd accused Royce of purposely making her look stupid and blamed him for ruining the choir's big night. He'd tried to explain that he never meant to do it, and he'd tried his best to hold back the laughter. He'd bitten his lip until it bled to stop it and had pointed to the cuts, but Mrs. Hildie had responded in a way that had stuck with him much longer than he'd expected.

"If that was the best you can do, then you shouldn't even try."

Aunt Tipsy had ripped into Mrs. Hildie in front of the principal the next morning, and Holly toilet papered her house the following weekend. As much as he appreciated their support, the damage was done. Royce didn't hear her words in his head as much anymore, but the sentiment still crept in from time to time, especially at the biggest moments in life where he stepped outside his comfort zone.

"Are you okay?" Sawyer's voice broke his contemplative silence and pulled him back to reality. "I don't think you've taken a single breath since we backed out of the driveway."

And maybe he hadn't. Royce pulled air deep into his lungs and calmed his jangling nerves with his next exhale. If only he'd learned that trick all those years ago. He could've given those families one hell of a show while singing Bob Dylan's "Blowin' in the Wind."

"Royce?"

Shaking himself out of it, he turned to look at Sawyer's handsome profile. "I'm deciding whether I want to cry or laugh."

"Oh God," Sawyer groaned. "Are you fixating on that middle school choir performance again?"

It was both a blessing and a curse to be married to someone who knew him so damn well. "Yep."

"Mrs. Hildie was a bitch." Sawyer's snarl and unwavering support made him smile. Reaching over the console, Sawyer took Royce's hand. "You can laugh, or you can cry. You can even do both at the same time. Just maybe not when the person from the family court does our home evaluation."

Royce laughed. "Fair enough."

"Want to tell me what triggered such an intense reaction?"

Royce looked at his husband as if he'd gone mad, but Sawyer kept his eyes on the road and didn't notice. "Darla is coming!"

"I know that, Paul Revere, but you've been really calm throughout the entire pregnancy. I expected to be the hysterical one."

"I never wanted to be a father until I met you. I didn't want to take a chance that my best wouldn't be good enough. It's one thing to mess up my life, but I never wanted to drag my kid through hell and back. It's bad enough I've made you an accessory to my fuckery." Royce pulled another deep breath into his lungs and exhaled slowly. "I never wanted to be a dad, and now it's the thing I want most in the entire world." Tears spilled down Royce's cheek, and he swallowed the lump that formed in his throat. "It's terrifying."

"I'd be more worried about us if we weren't scared out of our minds," Sawyer said. "Only an idiot goes into parenthood thinking they have all the answers."

Royce laughed abruptly. "True."

"We're going to make mistakes, but we have each other," Sawyer said. "I believe in you, Ro. You're going to be an incredible father."

"I won't be as good as you."

Waving him off, Sawyer said, "We'll be an unstoppable team. And when we falter, not if, we'll have the most loving village of humans to support us."

"Darla Grace Locke is going to be the luckiest little girl," Royce said.

"Damn right she is." Sawyer made a right turn into the hospital parking lot and followed the signs for labor and delivery.

"Pull over by the front entrance so we can unload our gear," Royce instructed. "I'll wait with it while you park."

"Maybe we should make sure they have a suite for us before we haul all of this upstairs," Sawyer said.

They'd toured the facility and were assured they'd have a private suite with Darla while Kelsey recovered in a separate room nearby. The hospital had limited space, and Kelsey's water broke four weeks early, so Royce conceded Sawyer's point. He grabbed the bag with the phone chargers, snacks, and a change of clothes for each of them. Once inside the hospital, they followed the signs to the labor and delivery unit. Well, one of them did. Royce's mind wandered again, and Sawyer snagged his sleeve anytime he headed in the wrong direction. The double glass doors to the maternity ward were kept locked, and Royce would've walked headfirst into them if not for Sawyer grabbing his elbow.

"Locked so people can't steal the babies, remember?" Sawyer teased.

"Get it together," Royce told himself.

Sawyer smirked and shook his head as he picked up the telephone receiver and provided their names and Kelsey's when prompted. The lock made an electric buzzing noise as soon as he returned the phone to its cradle, and they opened the doors and stepped inside.

A statuesque blonde nurse wearing Hello Kitty scrubs greeted them with a cheerful smile. "Hi. I'm Trinity. Kelsey told us to expect you. She's in room twelve, but she's getting changed into a couture hospital gown, so you might give her a minute."

"I can't tell if you're joking," Royce said. "Our girl is a fashionista, and I could see her ordering a custom gown for the big event."

"She brought her own gown when she delivered Ella," Sawyer said.

Trinity laughed. "I wasn't joking. She brought a pretty lilac hospital gown with her, and I wasn't about to tell her no."

Another nurse approached, older and with a stern countenance. "But I told her she's not getting a discount for bringing her own gown."

Royce waited for her to crack a smile, but none came. "Good to know," he replied.

"People are trying to sleep," Nurse Ratched said. From somewhere in the ward came a loud, snarly growl of a woman in the throes of labor. "Or deliver their babies in peace. Maybe you can get where you need to go instead of gabbing in the corridor."

Royce was twelve years old again, looking into the disapproving eyes of Mrs. Hildie.

"Oh, stuff it, Aggie," Trinity said. "They're not bothering anyone."

The older woman harrumphed and stomped away, her rubber-soled shoes squeaking in protest. Down the corridor, Andrew stepped out of a room and waved at them.

"Looks like Kels is ready for us," Sawyer said. "Thanks so much for your help."

"My pleasure," Trinity replied.

"Do we get to pick the nurse assigned to our suite?" Royce asked.

Trinity smiled sympathetically. "Sorry. We share duties in all the rooms, but I'll do my best to run interference. Aggie's actually a good person and a damn fine nurse, but she should've retired ten years ago."

The mother in labor let out another feral noise that made Royce's dick shrivel up inside him.

"I'd better go," Trinity said, bravely moving toward the scary sounds. "I'll check in with you soon and get you guys set up in your suite."

"Thank you," they called after her.

Andrew greeted them with bear hugs when they reached him. "Are you ready to meet your little girl?"

"So ready," Royce said.

"Your life is about to change in ways you never dreamed possible," Andrew told them.

Royce forced his eyes wide. "What goes on in the labor and delivery room?"

Andrew snorted and playfully slugged his shoulder. "Nothing scary." He cocked his head to the side. "Okay, some parts are, but this will still be the most beautiful moment of your life." Andrew scanned the only bag they'd brought up with them. "Is that it?"

"For now," Royce replied. "We didn't want to pack up all the stuff if our suite wasn't ready."

"Good thinking." Andrew leaned forward and sniffed. "Do you have snacks in there?"

Nodding, Royce said, "But we know the rules. If Kels can't eat in here, neither can we."

"Got that right," Kelsey called from inside. "Get in here. I need someone to watch television with me." They immediately answered her summons and entered the room to find her propped up in bed. She held a remote in one hand and a cup of ice in the other. "My water broke, but I've barely dilated a centimeter, and my cervix is still pretty thick. This might be a long night."

"No contractions?" Sawyer asked.

"Not so much as a twinge," Kelsey replied. "I did this with Ella, so I'm not surprised. Dr. Yang gave me the option of starting Pitocin to induce labor or waiting until her morning rounds to see if I'll transition on my own. Pitocin is the devil, so I'm going to wait."

Royce kissed her temple. "We want whatever is best for you."

"Be prepared for hours and hours of the *Housewives* franchise," Andrew cautioned.

"It's a small price to pay," Sawyer said.

Thirty minutes later, Royce couldn't decide if the antics intrigued or disgusted him. Kelsey explained the key differences between the shows, which extended beyond their location.

"All the shows follow affluent women," Kelsey said, "but the themes were different between the groups."

"There are Mormons participating in this?" Sawyer asked.

"In the Salt Lake City show. Some have left the church, and others follow the faith on their own terms," Kelsey said. "My favorite franchise is Atlanta, of course, since that's my hometown."

Aggie walked into the room, wearing a sour expression on her face. She checked the readout on the baby monitor before addressing Kelsey. "Still no contractions, huh?" Aggie's voice was much kinder than it had been in the hallway.

"Nope. She's going to be a stubborn one," Kelsey said.

Aggie nodded sympathetically before she turned and addressed the room. "I think it would be best if we cleared the room and let Kelsey get some rest while she still can."

"I have to go too?" Andrew asked.

"Yes, everyone," Aggie replied.

"But he's my husband," Kelsey said.

"And we're the baby's fathers," Sawyer protested.

Aggie smiled at this. "I'm not throwing you out of the hospital. I'm just asking you to congregate somewhere else."

"If you'll show us to our suite, Andrew can come hang out with us," Royce said.

"Where you'll eat snacks and party without me," Kelsey said with a cute pout.

"We're not going to have a rager, love," Andrew said. "We'll probably just watch ESPN."

"Fine. But I need you to set up story time first."

Andrew pulled a device from their bag and set it on a table. He pressed a button, and Royce's voice came through the speaker as he read *The Rainbow Fish*. He and Sawyer had recorded themselves reading a selection of books, some they'd even narrated together, so Kelsey could play them for Darla. They'd wanted her to get familiar with their voices while she was still in the womb.

Kelsey pushed a button on her bed to lower the head a little. She closed her eyes and sighed. "I might continue to play this every night at bedtime."

"Knocks us right out," Andrew told them. "If police work gets old, I think you guys have options."

"Ms. Rachel, we are not," Sawyer told him.

"You don't have to be," Kelsey said. "Maybe other kids with two dads or two moms would like to see themselves represented in a kids' show." She made a shooing motion at them. "You heard Aggie. I need my rest."

Andrew kissed his wife, lingering to whisper in her ear. They locked eyes when they pulled back, engaging in a silent conversation that put a smile on both their faces. Andrew winked at her and said, "Let's go, fellas."

"Can you imagine us creating a YouTube channel?" Royce said as they followed Aggie out of the room. "Then again, your carpet-cleaning buddy has probably made a mint."

"Is it James?" Aggie asked as she led them to the other side of the labor and delivery ward.

Royce groaned. "Not you too, Aggie."

She stopped outside a room and nodded at him. "Puts me right to sleep after a long twelve-hour shift."

"I knew you had good taste," Sawyer said.

Her countenance softened even more, but she held a finger to her lips. "Young families are sleeping, so please keep the noise to a minimum. I'll ask the same consideration of others when you two are adjusting to life with a newborn."

"We'll behave," Royce promised.

Aggie assessed him through narrowed eyes as if she'd correctly pegged him as the troublemaker.

Sawyer draped an arm around Royce's shoulders. "I'll make sure of it."

With that assurance, Aggie nodded once and left them to their own devices.

Andrew dropped into the recliner and immediately reached for the remote, earning a "this guy" look from Sawyer. Royce went straight for the snacks to settle his nerves. They'd brought an assortment of nutritious whole-grain foods and outright junk. It was only a matter of time before the jingling nerves from earlier settled in his stomach, so Royce reached for a granola bar with a sugar-free strawberry center instead of the chocolate chip cookies. The family suite was nice, but it wasn't spacious, so Royce put the room's other inhabitants' needs before his own by not getting an upset stomach. Andrew didn't suffer from the same compunction and reached for the bag of chocolate sandwich cookies.

"You can eat our food and hog our remote, but you're not stinking up our bathroom," Royce said.

Andrew shrugged. "Fair enough. Look, they're re-airing *The Ocho*," he said excitedly.

"What's that?" Sawyer asked.

"An event on ESPN8 where they feature the oddest competitions," Andrew replied. "We're talking dodgeball, extreme archery, and pillow fighting."

"They once had a mullet competition," Royce added.

"No way," Sawyer and Andrew said.

Royce chuckled as he sat at the foot of one hospital bed. "Yes, way. And outhouse racing too."

Sawyer sat beside him instead of taking the second bed. "I'm up for this."

"Me too," Andrew said as he popped out the footrest and reclined.

The three of them armchair quarterbacked one weird contest after another for the next hour until their phones chimed simultaneously with a group text notification.

Royce bolted upright from the bed with his heart in his throat. "Is it time?" he asked without checking the message.

Sawyer loosely wrapped a hand around Royce's wrist to keep him in place. "Relax. Kelsey isn't in labor."

"She's wide-awake and lonely," Andrew said, shutting the footrest and standing up. "I can't have that."

"Neither can we," Royce said. "She's putting herself through this for our benefit."

Sawyer stood up and laced his fingers through Royce's. "What's the plan for dodging Aggie on our way back to the delivery side of the ward?"

"We could just tell her that Kelsey doesn't want to be alone," Royce suggested.

"Kels tried that," Andrew said, reminding Royce that he still hadn't read the message. "Aggie told her she wasn't trying hard enough."

Royce released Sawyer's hand, retrieved his phone from the bed, and tapped the notification to read Kelsey's text.

Kelsey: Can't sleep. Lonely. Told Aggie I wanted my people back. She said I wasn't trying hard enough. I can sleep after Darla arrives. I need my people now.

Royce tucked his phone into his pocket. "One of us needs to create a diversion so the other two can sneak into her room. The diversionist can circle back and join us."

"Diversionist?" Andrew asked. "Is that a real word?"

"Yes," Sawyer replied. "And Royce is usually the man for the job, but he's in no shape to pull it off."

"Hey," Royce protested, even though he knew it was true.

Puffing out his chest, Andrew said, "I'll do it." He turned off the television and strode to the door, pausing at the threshold. "Tell my wife I love her if I don't make it back." Then Andrew disappeared from sight.

Royce and Sawyer stifled their laughter and followed, closing the door behind them. They trailed behind Andrew, who walked like a hero going into battle. When he made the last turn toward the delivery suites, Royce and Sawyer hung back at the corner. Sure enough, they heard Aggie's voice as she stopped Andrew before he reached Kelsey's room.

"So glad I ran into you," Andrew told her before launching into full diversion mode, asking her for directions and repeating them so badly that she had no choice but to show him the way.

They waited until Aggie's squeaking footsteps faded before they eased around the corner to find Trinity standing in the hallway with her arms crossed over her chest.

"Hiya," she said. "Whatcha doing?"

"Busted," Royce whispered.

Sawyer showed Trinity the text they'd received from Kelsey.

"Aww, bless her heart," the nurse said.

"Andrew acted as the diversion so we could sneak into Kelsey's room," Royce confessed.

Trinity snorted. "I knew something had to be up. No one is that bad with directions." She waved for them to follow her. "Kelsey's needs come first, and right now, that's her people." She moved with a general's confidence as she led them down the corridor. She knocked lightly on Kelsey's door and poked her head inside. "There are a few handsome fellas just dying to see you."

"Yes!" Kelsey hissed. "Send them in."

Trinity stepped aside so they could enter the room. "I'll go rescue your husband from Aggie."

"Did she put him in lockup?" Kelsey asked once Trinity left.

"She's just very protective of everyone's sleep and their need for quiet," Royce said. "The way she enforces her consideration could use some work."

Sawyer took the empty chair on the far side of the bed, and Royce wheeled a stool to the closest side. Andrew walked in a moment later, and the trio raised their hands and showered him with a whispered chorus of "Yay!"

Andrew pressed his hands to his face and struck a demure pose. "Who, me?"

"My hero," Kelsey said, clasping her hands to her heart.

Royce rolled the stool out of the way so Andrew could approach the bed.

Brushing the curls away from her face, Andrew searched her eyes. "Are you feeling okay?"

"I am now that my people are here." She puckered her lips, and Andrew kissed her softly. "Thank you."

"Anytime."

"Let's turn these lights up a little and play cards," Kelsey said.

Andrew removed a deck from her bag, but the only remaining chair was a recliner in the corner. They couldn't easily pull that up to her hospital bed, so they were figuring out logistics when Trinity returned with a rolling desk chair.

"You won't have to worry about Aggie bothering you unless you get too rowdy in here," the nurse said.

"We won't be a problem," Kelsey assured her. She turned on the television and set the volume low for background noise. "Rummy? Poker?"

"Go Fish is more my speed," Andrew said. "It's less cutthroat if everyone is honest."

"Rummy is cutthroat?" Sawyer asked.

Kelsey giggled. "It is in my family."

Andrew shuddered. "I still have the scars to prove it."

They played a few rounds of Go Fish before Kelsey suggested they switch to Uno. Andrew moaned softly but retrieved the deck from the bag.

"I can't wait to teach Ella the finer points of playing card games," Kelsey said.

"She'll be savage," Andrew replied. "No mercy for anyone."

"Not even us," Kelsey agreed.

Royce looked across the bed at Sawyer, who wore the dreamiest expression on his face. He knew his husband was picturing their future card game nights with their little family. Old Maid had been Royce's favorite as a kid because he'd learned how to read his opponents and use their weaknesses against them to rig the outcome in his favor, skills that still came in handy. Sawyer was just as analytical when playing cards, but he focused more on probabilities and statistics than human behavior. None of their prowess mattered because Kelsey trounced them all in four rounds.

Mild, sporadic contractions started around four in the morning, and Kels transitioned into active labor by six. Trinity and Aggie both came by just before seven to say they were leaving and to introduce the day shift nurses, Megan and Shannon. The contractions were consistent and looked extremely painful, but Kelsey breathed through them with Sawyer's help. Andrew massaged her feet, and Royce talked her through the peaks and valleys. At times, Royce's pulse matched the trajectory of each contraction on the graph, spiking at the little mountain peak and slowing as Kelsey's pain ebbed. Darla's precious heartbeat was the soothing soundtrack that kept him sane through it all.

"How are you doing with the pain?" Megan asked.

"Manageable," Kelsey said with a slight wince as a contraction peaked. "Don't need meds yet."

"Let me know if that changes," Megan told her as she studied her chart. "On paper, your labor is progressing perfectly. Contractions are increasing on cue as you get closer to the transition phase, but we don't really know how things are going unless we check your dilation. Looks like your cervix was fully effaced, and you were dilated to four centimeters when Trinity checked at five thirty. Dr. Yang will examine you when she comes in for rounds, so I won't check you now. It just increases the risk of infection, and no one wants that. Hit the call button if you need anything at all."

"I will," Kelsey assured her. She closed her eyes and rubbed a hand over her belly. "I don't need fingers in my cervix to know we're almost there, Lil Sketti Squash."

A surge of panic flooded through Royce. He casually leaned closer to the bed. "Are we talking minutes or hours?"

Kelsey giggled and patted his head. "She'll get here when she gets here." She opened one eye to look at him. "But I'd say two hours tops."

Royce glanced at the clock and noted that it was seven thirty. He kissed the back of Kelsey's palm and went back to studying the monitor for the next spike. Holy shit. Was he really just two hours away from meeting their daughter? Royce glanced over at his husband and found him looking just as shell-shocked.

"Two hours?" Sawyer mouthed.

Royce's head suddenly felt funny, and someone turned down the volume in the room. The edges of his vision grew fuzzy, and black dots danced in front of his eyes. Sawyer's mouth moved, but Royce couldn't hear the words for the weird buzzing noise. Was that a monitor? Was something wrong with Darla? He tried to claw his way through the fog, but he felt trapped. The harder he fought, the smaller his world became until his vision narrowed down to two tiny pinpricks. What the hell was happening to him? A hand landed on his shoulder, the touch warm and comforting. Sawyer's lips pressed to his ear, and a whisper of sound traveled through the canal to penetrate his brain.

"Breathe, baby." Sawyer's voice was a little louder this time, and it had the same magic effect as always.

As Royce's vision expanded, the room became brighter, and he noticed his pounding heart and restricted breathing. He sucked in a lungful of air and coughed.

"Easy," Sawyer cautioned, turning Royce's stool until they were eye to eye. He took Royce's hand and placed it over his heart. "Breathe with me. Nice and slow."

Royce closed his eyes and concentrated on the rise and fall of Sawyer's chest as he matched his breaths. Each inhale and exhale brought him back to his body until his awareness fully returned with embarrassment hot on its heels. He scanned the faces he loved and was relieved that he saw only concern or sympathy. "I don't know what just happened to me, but I didn't like it."

Kelsey reached over and patted his hand. "Sweetheart, you've realized your entire life is going to change in a few hours, and you had a minor panic attack."

"Are you sure?" Royce asked. "I've never experienced anything like that before."

"We're sure," Sawyer, Kelsey, and Andrew said.

But Royce wasn't convinced. "I think it was an alien abduction."

Kelsey snorted. "Drama queen."

"I recognize a panic attack when I see one," Sawyer said, using his strong fingers to massage the tension from Royce's neck.

"The same thing happened to Andrew," Kelsey said. "You're never as ready as you think you are."

"Her nursery is ready," Royce said. "We bought the best infant car seat on the market. Her clothes are clean and ready to go. We have diapers, butt cream, formula, and all the bottle stuff on hand. We're ready."

Andrew chuckled. "There's physically ready, and then there's emotionally ready. Buying all the stuff is the easy part." He tapped his temple. "Preparing this is an entirely different beast. About this time, panic sets in because you realize this tiny human will depend on you for their very existence and well-being. And just when you think you know what you're doing, life will throw you a curveball. Sleep schedules change, skin develops sensitivity to laundry detergents, and suddenly, they don't like the baby food they loved just the day before. You just roll with it, man. I won't tell you there's nothing to worry about. You're cops. You know there's everything to fear in this insane world, but you'll never be alone."

Royce turned to Sawyer and smiled. "We're ready. Not just the clothes and food. We can do this."

"It's a damn good thing because she's coming, ready or not," Kelsey said.

"Maybe you guys should go down to the cafeteria and grab a bite to eat while you still can," Andrew suggested. "Enjoy your last few hours as the dynamic duo."

"Nah," Royce said. "I wouldn't feel right about eating when Kelsey can't."

"Didn't stop you from stuffing snacks in your face," Kels said. "You reeked of powdery fake cheese when you came back to my room."

"Cheese puffs," Andrew told her.

"I hate those damn things, but I craved them as soon as I got a whiff of you three."

"Sorry," Sawyer said.

Kelsey tensed suddenly and looked down at her stomach. "Oh, I think I'll get to eat faster than I'd expected."

"What's that mean?" Sawyer asked.

Royce turned to the monitor and saw a huge contraction building. The damn thing looked like Mount Everest, and he turned to the bed to help coach Kelsey through the monster.

Kelsey gasped in the middle of Sawyer's breathing count and said, "I just felt Lil Sketti Squash move into position. Call the nurse."

CHAPTER FOUR

SAWYER'S BREATH CAUGHT IN HIS THROAT, AND HIS BRAIN screamed, "She's coming!" And judging by the shocked expressions around the room, he might've spoken the words out loud.

Kelsey's mouth curved into a grin before it contorted into a grimace. "I meant push the call button, not shout down the hallway."

Andrew ducked his head, but Sawyer didn't need to see his face to know he was laughing. The big guy's shoulders shook as he reached over the bed railing and pressed the call button.

Sawyer chuckled nervously. "I didn't mean to say that part out loud."

"She's coming?" Kelsey asked. "I could make so many jokes about that, but—" Her voice cut off suddenly, and she gritted out a guttural groan. "Fuck, that hurts."

Megan entered the room with a smile on her face. She cleared the call alert from a cell phone and tucked it into her pocket. "Everything okay in here?"

"I felt the baby drop into position, and there's a ton of pressure," Kelsey replied. "My body is telling me it's time to push."

"Okay," Megan said. "You breathe through the urge while I check things out." Megan pulled one corner of the blanket aside to give Kelsey privacy as she examined her. "Yep. You're fully dilated and ready to push." Megan looked at Sawyer and Royce. "Your little girl is eager to meet her dads."

"Holy shit. This is really happening," Royce whispered.

"Uh-huh," Sawyer replied.

"Here's what we're going to do," Megan said. "I'm going to call Dr. Yang and let her know you're ready for her. Then I'm going to get the bed ready for the next stage. I need you to keep breathing through the contractions and resist the urge to push, okay?"

Kelsey nodded vigorously. "Yes."

"Help her stay calm and focused," Megan instructed the men.

"Here comes another contraction, baby," Andrew said.

"Really?" Kelsey asked dryly as her stomach tensed.

"Slow, deep breaths, Kels," Sawyer said. "You've got this."

Megan spoke calmly but urgently into the phone as she removed the lower half of the bed. She pulled the stirrups into position and locked them into place. Megan tucked her phone back into her pocket and said, "I'll stand right here in case of an emergency. Everything is going to be just fine."

"Have you ever delivered a baby before?" Royce asked.

"Once at a shopping mall," Megan replied. "I'd much rather be in this situation than that one."

"I bet."

Emotions surged inside Sawyer like a tidal wave, and he wasn't sure what to do with them. He threaded his fingers through Kelsey's and then kissed the back of her hand. "What can I do to help?"

"Just stay right there. I have my best guys by my side, and I can do anything."

Royce sucked in air between his teeth and shook his head sadly at Andrew. "Such a tough way to find out you share the top spot with two others. Ouch."

"With a woman like Kelsey, I'll take anything she gives me and be damn grateful for it," Andrew said.

Sawyer admired Royce's ability to ease the rising tension in the room with jokes.

Kelsey must've appreciated it, too, because she kissed Andrew between contractions, cupped his cheek, and said, "You'd get so lucky tonight if I weren't about to split my vagina in half."

Andrew grimaced, Royce sucked in a sharp breath, and Sawyer cast a wary glance at the end of the bed to where Megan stood with a smile on her face. At least she was enjoying their friendly banter.

Royce crossed his legs and leaned forward a little. "Split in half?"

"Sure feels that way," Kelsey said.

Sawyer was overcome with remorse. "I'm so sorry. I knew pregnancy came with a host of uncomfortable side effects and that delivery would be painful, but it sounds like medieval torture."

"It's okay." Kelsey inhaled deeply as the next contraction built, and the breath exhaled shakily. "I'm tough, and I knew what I was volunteering for." She squeezed his hand and tugged him down closer. "I fucking love you, and this has been an absolute—" She sucked in air into her lungs. "Holy shit, this little girl wants out now."

"Do you hear that?" Royce asked proudly. "Our Darla Grace is raising hell already."

Dr. Yang came in at that exact moment. "Sounds like I got here just in time."

"Yes!" Kelsey exclaimed. "I'm going to evacuate their little angel, and my man is going to get me something delicious to eat."

"Nah, your first meal is on us," Royce said. "You tell us what you want, and we'll make sure it arrives."

"Pancakes," Kelsey said as Dr. Yang donned her protective gear. "No, make that french toast. Or maybe sausage gravy and biscuits." Her body tensed with another contraction. "I don't think I can hold this one off."

"Let's just breathe through this last one," Dr. Yang said as she stood at the foot of the bed and positioned Kelsey's legs in the stirrups. "On your next contraction—"

"Big breath, chin to chest, and bear down for ten seconds," Kelsey replied.

"That's right."

"Dads, do you want to hide at the top of the bed with Kelsey or stand down here to see your little girl enter the world?" Dr. Yang asked.

"Umm," they both replied. Sawyer and Royce had prepared for everything but where to position themselves during delivery.

"It's okay with me if you stand down there," Kelsey said. "I'd invite anyone to the show at this point."

Royce snickered and positioned himself by Kelsey's knees, but Sawyer stayed in place to hold her hand while she pushed their baby girl into the world. "You've got a cute vagina, Kels."

Andrew snorted and shook his head. "You're such an idiot, but I love you."

Sawyer aimed a disbelieving glare at Royce, who merely shrugged.

"Aww, shucks," Kelsey said. "Thank you. I'm quite fond of her too."

"I'm also a big fan," Andrew told her.

"You'll have six weeks to write her poems," Kelsey teased.

"Here comes your next contraction," Dr. Yang said. "Ready."

Kelsey inhaled a deep breath and nodded.

"Push," Dr. Yang said.

Sawyer immediately started counting down from ten as Kelsey bore down and pushed.

"You've got this, baby," Andrew said as he placed a hand on her back.

"You're doing great, Kelsey," Dr. Yang said. She reached for an instrument, and Royce scurried back up the bed, looking wild-eyed, pale, and wobbly. "I'll only need to make a slight cut to ease her way."

"Okay," Kelsey said meekly.

Royce made scissors with his two fingers and mimed cutting. He shivered hard and nearly went down. Sawyer grabbed his arm with his free hand and held on until Royce's legs steadied.

"One more push and she'll be here," Dr. Yang told them. "She has tons of dark hair."

Sawyer's heart had never pounded so hard, and he feared he would pass out if he didn't calm down. He took a steadying breath because he would not miss this moment. Sawyer glanced over at the monitor as another contraction started. "Here we go, Kels. One more big push."

Kelsey took a big breath and bore down one last time.

"Here comes her head," Dr. Yang said.

Royce moved back to Kelsey's knees and watched, his hand covering his mouth. Tears rolled down his face, and he turned and met Sawyer's gaze. "She has so much hair."

"Her head is clear. Just a little more effort and her shoulders will be free," Dr. Yang encouraged.

Kelsey released a feral growl, pushing with everything she had.

"And here she is," Dr. Yang said.

Sawyer looked at the foot of the bed in time to see the doctor holding Darla. Her arms waved angrily in the air, and her tiny cries filled the room. Their baby girl was a gooey mess but still the most beautiful sight Sawyer had ever seen.

Kelsey relaxed back against the bed and released a choked sob. "We did it."

Sawyer leaned forward and kissed her temple. "No, *you* did it."

"Would you like to cut the cord?" Dr. Yang asked Royce.

"Yes, please."

They'd planned this moment. Royce would cut the cord, and Sawyer would do the first round of skin-to-skin bonding. Sawyer watched as his husband accepted the scissors from the doctor and cut Darla's umbilical cord as instructed. The nursing team took Darla from Dr. Yang to clean and assess her, and Royce followed closely on their heels. They didn't go far, just to the infant warmer at the opposite corner of the room.

Royce looked over his shoulder and called out, "Ten fingers. Ten toes. Enough hair for five baby girls. Evangeline will buy every baby hair accessory under the sun."

Kelsey giggled, pulling Sawyer's attention to her. She watched the activity with a look of absolute pride on her face. There were so many things he wanted to say, but nothing came out when he opened his mouth to speak. Sawyer lifted Kelsey's hand to his mouth and kissed the back of it instead as tears streamed down his face. Joy and gratitude bubbled to the surface like the finest champagne and burst from him in a broken sob. Kelsey turned to look at him, her eyes filling with tears when their gazes collided. "I…" Sawyer shook his head. Christ, he'd considered himself an eloquent person up to that point, but he couldn't get a single word past the lump of emotions in his throat.

Kelsey freed her other hand from Andrew's and cupped Sawyer's face. "I know."

Royce and the nurses laughed across the room, and Sawyer wondered what adorable moment he'd just missed. But he was torn between his little miracle and the woman who made her existence a reality. Royce looked over his shoulder again, and their eyes connected.

"She just pooped and peed on the nurses," Royce announced proudly. "Her waste disposal systems are a go."

Sawyer pulled himself together and looked into Kelsey's soulful brown eyes again. "Thank you, thank you, thank you. I'll never be able to express my thanks enough."

"A shiny new Range Rover would be a nice token of appreciation," Andrew teased.

Kelsey dismissed him with a wave. "Don't listen to him. This experience has meant the world to me, and I'm so grateful I got to be a part of it. I cannot wait to see the remarkable person Darla grows up to be." More laughter came from Royce and the nurses. "Go meet your little girl. It sounds like she's already causing a ruckus."

Sawyer leaned forward once more and kissed her forehead. "I love you so damn much."

"I love you too. Can I come meet her after I eat and get some rest?"

"Of course. Whenever you're ready." But Sawyer was still reluctant to leave Kelsey.

"I've got her from here," Andrew promised him.

Sawyer nodded, released Kelsey's hand, and stepped away. "Did you decide what you want to eat for breakfast? Pancakes, french toast, or biscuits and gravy."

"Yes, please," Kelsey said with a giggle. "Surely, I need to replenish calories after childbirth."

Sawyer chuckled. "We'll hook you up. Text us your room number once you get moved."

"They'll let me rest and recover here for a bit before moving me over. You can just put my name on the order, and someone from the desk downstairs will call up to labor and delivery. Andrew can go down and get it."

"Is there anything special you want?" Sawyer asked Andrew.

"Nah, I'll eat anything."

"I'll place the order as soon as they move us to our suite. Love you, guys."

"Love you," Kelsey and Andrew echoed.

Sawyer joined Royce and the nurses across the room. He looped his arms around Royce's shoulders, and Royce slid his arm around Sawyer's waist. They stared down at their perfect angel, who blinked beneath the warmer's bright lights. Darla's limbs were long and lean just like her mother's. Her skin was pink from getting toweled off, but the beautiful, warm brown tone of her skin was evident beneath the blush. Sawyer couldn't resist counting Darla's fingers and toes as the nurses prepared to swaddle her. He was dying to see her hair for himself too, but they'd already put a hat on her tiny head to help regulate her temperature. He'd wait to sneak a peek once they got moved to their own room.

"We just finished her second Apgar test, and she scored great," Megan said.

"Our brilliant baby girl," Sawyer said. "How much does she weigh?"

Royce rested his head against Sawyer's shoulder. "Seven pounds and two ounces. I've probably taken two dozen pictures already, and she's about ten minutes old."

"She's twenty inches long," Megan added.

"That's incredible, considering she arrived four weeks early," Sawyer said.

Darla's tiny bow mouth opened, and she made her opinion about their conversation known.

"She has those healthy Locke lungs too," Royce said. "Never afraid to speak their minds."

Megan laughed as she finished the swaddle and transferred Darla to a bassinet attached to a chest of drawers on wheels. "Are you guys ready to head over to your suite?"

"Yes," Sawyer and Royce said.

They called out their goodbyes to Andrew and Kelsey before following Megan out of the room.

"We need to order a breakfast fit for a queen," Sawyer said.

Royce whipped out his phone. "Leave it to me." He tapped and scrolled for the duration of the walk. "How do we make sure she gets it? There's a box here for delivery driver instructions."

Sawyer repeated what Kelsey had told him.

Royce typed for a few moments, tapped once more, and grinned with satisfaction. "I added food for us and treats for the nursing staff too."

"Bless you," Megan said as she entered their suite. "Which one of you is going to take the first shift of skin-to-skin bonding?"

Sawyer whipped off his shirt before she finished the question. "Me."

Megan blinked a few times, turned a cute shade of pink, and

shifted her attention to the baby. "You make yourself comfortable, and I'll bring her over to you."

Sawyer sat down on the love seat, and Royce joined him. Megan carefully unwrapped Darla, who immediately cried to protest the loss of warmth.

"I have something better for you, sweetheart," Megan said as she carried Darla over. "You want her tummy against your chest. We recommend thirty minutes twice a day for the first few weeks of her life, but some experts recommend the practice for longer. Feeding times are the easiest."

Sawyer's heart was in his throat, and his hands shook as he accepted the crying baby from Megan. "I've got you, sweetheart. Daddy's here." He gently placed Darla against his chest and covered her with her little blanket. "I've been waiting for you forever." Darla calmed immediately and made the cutest little newborn noises he'd ever heard. Sawyer let peace wash over him and prayed for time to slow down.

Royce stroked his finger over the tiny fist resting against Sawyer's chest. "What a blessing."

"So sweet," Megan said. "I'm going to head back over to my side of the unit. Your new nursing team will check in with you soon to get her ready for her first feeding. They'll also go over basic newborn care." She smiled warmly. "Looks to me like you're both pros already."

"We're involved godfathers and uncles," Royce explained. "We're no stranger to diapers, bottle feedings, and anything else this little girl might throw our way."

Megan smiled brilliantly. "Nothing left to do but settle in and get to know your baby girl."

"Thank you for everything," Sawyer told her.

"It was my pleasure."

Sawyer had mostly held his emotions in check while Megan was in the room, but tears flooded his eyes the moment she stepped outside and closed the door. "I can't believe she's finally here." The tears ran unchecked down his face. Sawyer swiped them away, but new ones immediately took their place. "I can't turn these darn things off. Can you find the faucet and give it a hard crank?"

Royce got up on his knees, wrapped one arm around Sawyer's shoulder, and carefully draped the other under Darla, pulling them into a family hug. He pressed a kiss into Sawyer's hair and on top of Darla's head before whispering, "Cry as much as you want to. This is the biggest moment in our life." Royce's voice was thick with tears too, and Sawyer felt the way Royce's body trembled against his.

Sawyer leaned into Royce's warmth and rested his head against Royce's shoulder. "She's so perfect."

"Gorgeous, just like her mom," Royce agreed. "And she has so much hair. Kels will have to teach us the proper way to care for those glorious curls."

"I didn't get to see her hair," Sawyer said, not bothering to keep the pout from his voice.

"Take a peek."

"I want to, but I don't want to let any of her body heat out."

"We'll be fast," Royce said. "Then I'll cover you both with my favorite blanket Aunt Tipsy knitted."

"Okay, but quickly."

Royce reached over and gently peeled the knitted cap off her head to reveal thick, dark curls. "Evangeline is going to go nuts over this hair."

Sawyer longed to run his fingers over the silky strands but resisted the urge. "Okay, cover her back up. It feels cold in here."

"That's because our little angel is stealing all your body heat."

"Worth it," Sawyer said as he shivered.

Royce positioned the hat back in place and retrieved the soft blanket from the bag. "Lean forward." Sawyer did as instructed, and Royce draped it around his shoulders and crisscrossed the material over his chest, leaving Darla's head sticking out of the little cocoon. "How's that?"

"Better if you were in here with us. This blanket is certainly big enough."

"Let me reach out to Ivy first, and then I'll climb under there with you."

"Can you do a quick group text to our friends and family to let them know Darla is here too?" Sawyer asked.

"Yep. Ivy first so she can get our legal documentation filed, then friends and family. I know just the first picture I want to send them."

Royce called Ivy first and left a voicemail message when she didn't answer. Then he sent out their birth announcement before switching his text notifications to vibration so they wouldn't disturb their little miss. Dozens of messages flooded in within seconds, everyone congratulating them and expressing their excitement to meet Darla. Evangeline and Eddie wanted to know when they could come to the hospital, and Royce replied that he'd get back to them in a few hours.

Sawyer lifted a corner of the blanket in invitation, and Royce slid inside the toasty cocoon. "I have never felt this at peace with the world."

"Me neither." Then Royce tilted his head to the side. "Or I will be as soon as Ivy confirms she sent the post-birth agreement to the judge."

"I'm sure she'll get back to us soon."

But before they knew it, hours had passed. They'd consumed

their breakfast and made sure Kelsey got hers. She'd responded with a picture of her buffet spread around her and a second picture of Andrew eating a single strawberry and wearing a sad face. A nurse named Kitty had assisted them with Darla's first feeding. Their Lil Pumpkin had been sleepy and shown little interest in eating. Kitty had assured him that some babies just wanted to be left alone after their big arrival. Darla took almost an ounce with patient coaxing, and the nurse accepted that for her first feeding. Kitty had made sure they were comfortable changing her diaper and had given them a thumbs-up when they'd completed the task. They'd get additional training before they took Darla home, which reminded Sawyer that they hadn't heard from Ivy yet.

Sawyer reluctantly placed Darla back in her bassinet and turned to Royce. "Should we call Ivy again? Or maybe try her office. Someone else could surely file the paperwork on our behalf if she's tied up in court today."

"It's worth a shot." Royce pulled up Ivy's contact on his phone and called the office. He pursed his lips as he waited, then said, "It's going to voicemail too. This is Thursday, right?"

"Yep." Sawyer checked his time on his watch. "It's too early for them to close for lunch if that's their practice."

Royce left a voicemail message at the office and then texted Ivy's cell phone for good measure. "I'm sure we'll hear from her soon. Do you want to take a nap while Darla sleeps, or should we reach back out to our parents and let them know when they can come visit?"

Sawyer sighed heavily. "I'm not sure I'll be able to sleep after so much excitement." But his mouth parted on a jaw-cracking yawn that contradicted him. "Maybe a little nap." He looked at the two hospital beds. "Do you have a preference?"

Royce snorted. "I'm getting in your bed and spooning you, so pick one."

"Here? What if a nurse comes in to check on us?"

"We won't be naked, and Kitty said they'd mostly leave us alone unless we called for them. We have plenty of diaper supplies and baby formula. Kitty posted Darla's feeding schedule for us, so there's no reason for them to come in."

"Bring that blanket," Sawyer said as he headed toward the closest bed. His feet grew heavier with each step he took. Just maybe he could shut his eyes and catch a quick nap.

They settled into the bed with Royce spooning behind him. Sawyer lay facing the bassinet, where he could stare at their little angel until he dropped off to sleep. Royce had no issues nodding off. He was out as soon as his head hit the pillow. Ninety-nine percent of Sawyer wanted to doze off too, but that one percent kept his lids open and his mind focused on the one thing that hadn't gone according to their carefully laid plans.

Where the hell was Ivy, and why wasn't she returning their messages?

CHAPTER FIVE

SAWYER TORE HIS WORRIED GAZE AWAY FROM THEIR DAUGHTER and looked at Royce with pleading eyes. "I don't think she likes me. Maybe you should try to feed her."

"Doesn't like you?" Royce scoffed. "Darla slept against your chest for a solid hour. Our daughter is completely smitten with you, just like everyone else who meets you." Sawyer raised a cynical eyebrow. "I'm serious. You heard what Kitty said about newborns. They don't all slide from their mother's womb and knock back the milk like little pros. Some babies take more coaxing."

Sawyer looked at their sleeping daughter and back to Royce again. "I hear you. I really do, but do you mind trying to feed her?"

"Of course not." Royce slid his arm under Darla for the transfer. "Hi there, Pumpkin. I missed you." He ran the bottle's nipple over her bottom lip, and she opened her mouth to latch on.

"See," Sawyer whispered. "She likes you better."

Darla attempted to drink for a few seconds but then pulled away and cried like she was in pain. Just like she'd done during her first feeding and again with Sawyer.

"Do you think something is wrong?" Sawyer asked. "She appears to be hungry."

Royce furrowed his brow as he soothed her. "I'm not sure. Is she hungry or pissed we're waking her up?"

"Should we call a nurse?" Sawyer asked.

Royce checked the time on the clock. "The grandparents are due to arrive any minute now. I think we should continue coaxing her to drink like Kitty showed us until after they leave."

"Okay."

Sawyer sat down beside him and gently brushed his fingers over Darla's forehead. Her skin smoothed out, and she stopped crying. "Maybe she likes me a little."

Royce kissed his cheek. "She loves you a lot."

They worked in tandem, soothing and coaxing Darla to drink until a knock sounded at the door. Royce held up the small, single-use bottle of formula to check her progress. "We managed an ounce in thirty minutes."

Sawyer stood up and recorded the stats on the chart before answering the door. Eddie and Evangeline stood on the other side, grinning like lunatics. "Hey. Come in and meet your granddaughter."

The hospital allowed just two visitors in the room at a time. There was no doubt in anyone's mind that Evangeline would be one of the first to visit Darla, and Royce was curious how Eddie had finagled the second spot. "Is Barron tied up somewhere?"

Evangeline rolled her eyes on her way to the sink to wash her hands. Afterward, she paused long enough to kiss Sawyer's cheek before easing down beside Royce on the sofa and leaning in to get the first peek of her sleeping granddaughter. "Oh, my heart. She's so beautiful," she whispered. "Hello, angel."

Eddie gave Sawyer a bear hug and walked to the sink to wash up too. "Barron was a perfect gentleman who volunteered his spot since we all knew Evangeline would get first dibs."

"I know that's right," she said.

Eddie squatted down in front of Royce and smiled when he laid eyes on Darla. "What a beauty."

Darla opened her eyes and blinked up at Eddie.

Evangeline giggled. "She's batting those long, dark eyelashes at her grandpa already."

Chuckling, Eddie ran the back of his finger over her downy cheek and smiled at the little girl, who seemed completely enthralled by him. "Are you going to be my best girl?"

"As if anyone can resist the Locke charm," Evangeline said with a snort. "Eddie, shall we do rock, paper, scissors to see which one of us gets to hold her first?"

Eddie tore his gaze away from Darla to smirk at Evangeline. "The honor is all yours."

Evangeline placed a hand over her heart. "You're such a gentleman."

"Nah, I just don't want to wear a bloody stump for the rest of my life."

Evangeline laughed gleefully, and Darla blinked in response. After rubbing her hands together in delight, Evangeline opened her arms so Royce could transfer her granddaughter to them. "Oh, how I've prayed for this day." Evangeline stared down at Darla's face and ran her fingers over the tiny fist that had worked its way out of the swaddling. She sniffled and gently swayed from side to side. "How I've prayed for you."

"She's really something," Eddie said. "I can't wait to see what's hiding under her little cap."

"Curls for days," Royce replied.

Evangeline snapped her head up. "Really? Can I have a little peek?"

Royce reached over and removed the knit hat to show off Darla's black hair. The volume made him laugh. Eddie and Evangeline oohed and aahed until he replaced the hat.

"She's absolutely precious," Evangeline said. "And seems so peaceful."

"Until you try to feed her," Sawyer said. "She gets feisty then."

"Some babies are pretty lethargic after birth," Evangeline replied. "How many times have you tried to feed her?"

"Just twice. She managed only an ounce this last time."

"Is she latching on?" Evangeline asked.

"Seems to, or at least the instinct is there," Royce replied.

"Harper was a fussy eater," Eddie told them. "I had pretty good luck with him. Want me to try?"

The offer warmed Royce's heart. "Maybe if you're here for her next feeding." He checked the clock to gauge when that would be and realized it was already two o'clock, and they still hadn't heard from Ivy or anyone else at her firm. What was taking them so long? Royce tried to set aside his rising frustration and enjoy the visit with their family.

"You might have the nurse or pediatrician make sure she doesn't have a tongue tie," Evangeline said. "I'd take a peek, but I don't want to make her mad at me. Sawyer needed a lingual frenectomy when he was a baby. It's pretty common."

"What's a tongue tie?" Eddie asked.

Evangeline opened her mouth and rolled her tongue back to expose the band of tissue connecting her tongue to the floor of her mouth. "Sometimes they're too thick or too short, and it doesn't allow the tongue to move. Darla might struggle to latch onto the nipple properly, or she could be in pain when she does."

71

Sawyer moved over and stared down at their daughter. "I don't want her to be in any pain. Maybe we should call the nurse to find out when Dr. Edwards is going to get here for her initial visit."

Royce stood up and said, "I need to stretch my legs and make a phone call. I'll head over to the nurses' station and ask." Sawyer's eyes darted to the clock, and Royce knew he was worried sick about the lack of communication. Healthy newborns were often sent home a day, sometimes two, after their delivery. If Darla checked off all the boxes, the pediatrician could sign off on sending her home, but they couldn't take her from the hospital without the legal documents. It wouldn't do either of them any good to get worked up, so he sent reassuring vibes Sawyer's way. "I'll be right back."

"Okay."

He'd almost reached the nurses' station when Eddie caught up with him.

"Sawyer told us what's going on with the lawyer," Eddie said. "How can I help?"

"I'm not sure. We've only managed a catnap after being up all night, and my brain isn't firing on all cylinders. I stepped out here to figure something out."

"Call your lawyer again now. If you don't get an answer, I'll drive over there and talk to someone." When Royce opened his mouth to protest, Eddie raised his hands. "I won't raise hell or embarrass you. I'll just make sure someone there knows that Darla was born this morning and you guys need them to send the legal paperwork to the courthouse." He cocked his head to the side. "Does Kelsey's lawyer have copies of the same paperwork?"

"I don't know, Eddie. Maybe. They'd have copies of everything we signed, and they'd get copies of the documents filed in court. I doubt they'd file the papers on our behalf. Miguel doesn't represent us."

"Good point. I didn't think of that."

"Besides, I don't want to disturb Kelsey right now. She's supposed to come for a visit after she's rested."

"Was her delivery tough?" Eddie asked.

"I think they all are. Damn, I can't imagine how painful that is."

Eddie grimaced in sympathy. "Will you give her a great big hug from me when you see her?"

"See who?" Kelsey asked from behind them.

Royce and Eddie turned around to greet Kelsey and Andrew. She'd changed into lilac pajamas with a matching fuzzy robe, slippers, and headband to keep her curls out of her face. If Royce hadn't seen her give birth hours before, he wouldn't have believed it. The presence of a wheelchair was the only hint that she'd been through something. He couldn't say the same for Andrew, who, though still handsome, looked like he'd been dragged to hell and back. Royce figured his condition resembled Andrew's current state than Kelsey's.

"Sweetheart, how do you manage to look so beautiful just a few hours after giving birth?" Eddie asked her.

"Nice distraction ploy, Eddie. Are you stepping out on me?"

"Never, gorgeous," Eddie replied. He leaned down and gently hugged her. "You're one hell of a woman."

Kelsey patted his back. "I know."

Eddie shook Andrew's hand and clasped him on the shoulder. "Good to see you again."

"Likewise, sir," Andrew said.

"Are you just now moving over here?" Royce asked.

Kelsey grinned sheepishly. "Baby doll, I ate that feast you bought for us, turned on my bedtime stories, and conked out for hours. The nurses must not have needed my room because they left me alone."

She released an enormous yawn and sighed. "I think I'm ready for another round."

"Food or nap?" Royce asked.

Kelsey laughed but then winced and placed a hand on her stomach. "Both."

"I'd imagine so," Eddie said. "Can I get something for you?"

"My mom is bringing food soon," Andrew said. "But thank you."

"How's Darla?" Kelsey asked.

"She's getting her first lessons in world domination from Evangeline," Royce replied. He briefly debated telling her about the situation with Ivy but decided against it. She deserved to rest peacefully. He'd tell her there was a problem if he identified one existed.

Kelsey narrowed her eyes and studied him closely. "Then why are the two of you out here?"

"I needed to stretch my legs, and I have a question for the nursing staff," Royce replied.

She cocked her head to the side. "You would tell me if there was something wrong, wouldn't you?"

"Of course."

Kelsey shook her head and sighed. "I know there's stuff you're not telling me, but I'm honestly too tired to interrogate you further. You're safe for now." She looked over her shoulder at Andrew. "To our recovery suite, Big Sexy."

Andrew saluted Eddie and Royce with two fingers before wheeling her past them.

"Love you, Kels," Royce called out.

"Love you more," she replied.

They stayed put until Andrew wheeled her out of sight, then Eddie leaned in and whispered, "She's scarily perceptive."

Royce nodded his agreement. "And I better have some solid answers the next time I see her."

"Try the lawyer's office again," Eddie suggested.

Ivy's cell phone and the office line went to voicemail. Royce texted her, even though he didn't expect to have a different result from his previous attempts.

"Nothing?" Eddie asked.

"Nada." Royce tucked his phone away and blew out a frustrated breath. "I'm going to take you up on your generous offer. I don't want to leave Sawyer and Darla, and I'm in no shape to drive. Do you promise to be polite if you're able to talk to someone at Ivy's office?"

Eddie clasped his shoulder. "I promise I won't fuck this up for you, son. You take care of your little girl and let me see what's going on at the law firm."

His father's steady gaze calmed his nerves. "Okay. I appreciate it."

"Do you mind if Jo hangs around here until I get back?"

"Of course not. Send her back so she can meet Darla."

They exchanged a fierce hug before going their separate ways. Royce's spirit felt much lighter as he approached the nurses' station.

Kitty looked up from her computer and smiled. "Is everything okay?"

"Maybe not," Royce replied honestly. "Darla wasn't interested in eating again. She tries to latch on or acts like she wants to, but cries when she tries to drink from her bottle. Like maybe she's frustrated or hurting. Do you know when Dr. Edwards is expected to arrive?"

"Aww, bless her heart," Kitty said. "Dr. Edwards is here now, visiting her newest patients. You should be next."

Royce rapped his knuckles against the counter. "Perfect. Thank you."

"Is there anything else I can get you?"

"No, but thank you."

Kitty leaned forward and lowered her voice. "Was that Evangeline O'Neal I saw entering your suite?"

Royce laughed. "Yes, she's my mother-in-law." The nurse blinked rapidly for a few minutes, and he could see her doing the math. Evangeline didn't look old enough to be Sawyer's mother, but he wasn't even her oldest kid. Royce knew better than to say that part out loud. "She has fantastic genetics and probably mystical powers," he whispered to Kitty.

She laughed. "I believe it."

"You should stop in and meet her. She's lovely."

"Oh, I couldn't. Not without spending an hour in the locker room to do my hair and makeup."

Royce waved her off. "She's not pretentious like that. No one makes you feel better about yourself than Evangeline."

Kitty tilted her head as if considering his words. "Maybe if things stay quiet." Her phone rang, and she pointed at it. "Just jinxed myself."

"Good luck," he said before walking away.

A tall Black woman in a lab coat stopped outside their suite as Royce approached. They'd only met her once when they were interviewing potential pediatricians, but they'd been drawn to her warm nature immediately. "I hear congratulations are in order."

"Thank you, Dr. Edwards," he said. "I'm so glad you're here."

She arched a brow. "Is everything okay?"

"We're concerned that Darla either doesn't want to drink or wants to but can't." Royce opened the door and gestured for her to enter first. "We'll feel much better after you've examined her."

Sawyer greeted Dr. Edwards warmly and stood up to shake her hand. Royce stepped into the room and closed the door. Evangeline was too focused on her granddaughter to notice anything else.

"And you can be anyone you want to be, my love," Evangeline said to the sleeping infant in her arms. "You can travel wherever you want to. Love whoever you want to. The sky is your limit."

Sawyer placed a hand on his mother's back. "I hate to interrupt, but Darla's pediatrician is here to examine her newest patient."

Dr. Edwards held out her hands and said, "May I?"

Evangeline tightened her hold ever so slightly before relinquishing her granddaughter with an exaggerated sigh. "If you must."

Sawyer chuckled and hugged his mother. "I'm so glad you're here."

Returning his squeeze, Evangeline said, "Where else would I be?"

Someone knocked on the door, and Jo pushed it open enough to poke her head into the room. "Eddie said I could come on back." She saw Dr. Edwards at the bassinet with Darla. "Oh, should I come back in a bit?"

"Not on my account," Dr. Edwards said.

"Come on in," Royce said.

Jo stepped inside and shut the door. She hugged the guys before embracing Evangeline. "This is so exciting." She clasped her hands together in front of her. "It's been a while since I've held a baby. I might be rusty."

"It's like riding a bike," Evangeline said. "She's so sweet and cuddly. I practically snarled at the doctor when she asked to examine her."

Royce and Sawyer eased closer to Dr. Edwards without crowding her. She examined Darla from head to toe, talking sweetly to her every step of the way. Darla would open her eyes occasionally or fuss her displeasure at being disturbed. She formed a moue with her little bow mouth, furrowed her brow, or scrunched her cheeks in protest.

"Your little girl has opinions," Dr. Edwards said.

"Good," they replied.

Dr. Edwards laughed as she swaddled Darla once more, and the baby settled immediately. "Who gets her?"

"Can I hold her now?" Jo asked Evangeline. "I might just burst otherwise."

"I'll share her with you," Evangeline replied.

"Yes!" Jo practically Tigger-bounced over to the sink to wash her hands.

"What about her fathers?" Sawyer asked.

His mother grinned. "Eh, maybe."

Jo took the sleeping bundle from Dr. Edwards and carefully crossed to the sofa. The grandmothers fussed over Darla, and the guys turned their attention to what the doctor had to say.

"She definitely has a tongue tie, and it's my opinion that she would benefit from a procedure to correct it. But we need to consult certified lactation consultants and speech pathologists first." Dr. Edwards looked at the feeding chart and noted the time of her next bottle. "I'll make sure both are on hand to observe her next feeding, and if they agree with my assessment, I'll perform the procedure early tomorrow morning." She described the frenectomy in enough detail to make Royce's stomach pitch, while Sawyer gripped his hand hard enough to snap bones. "I know it sounds awful, but I will give her a small amount of anesthesia to numb the area, and her recovery time will be minimal. We might have to keep your darling at the hospital for an extra day for observation to make sure she's latching on properly and taking a bottle well."

"Thank you so much," Royce said.

"My pleasure."

Once Dr. Edwards left, Royce turned to Sawyer. "This might buy us some extra time to figure out what's going on with Ivy. Hopefully, Eddie's mission is successful."

"Where'd Eddie go?" Evangeline asked.

"He's driving over to our lawyer's office to see what's going on," Royce explained. "He's going to make sure someone at the law office calls us."

"Should've sent me," Evangeline said. The menacing scowl on her face told Royce he'd made the right decision to send Eddie instead, something he never thought he'd say.

"Whoa, killer," Sawyer told his mother.

Royce was on the verge of telling Evangeline not to jump to conclusions when his phone rang. A glance at it showed Eddie's name on the caller ID. Royce accepted the call and said, "Have any luck?"

"I couldn't get in," Eddie said. "The place is swarming with cops."

Royce froze in fear. "Cops?"

"What's going on?" Sawyer whispered, but Royce only had enough functioning brain cells to concentrate on one conversation at a time. He held up his finger and asked Sawyer to wait.

"Yeah," Eddie said. "They've barricaded the parking lot, so no one can get in there. I approached on foot to ask some questions, but the sheriff's deputy wasn't in a chatty mood. He sent my ass packing."

"Sheriff's deputy?" Royce asked. "Why were the county boys there? The law office is within city limits."

"Beats me, but there were more county boys there than city," Eddie said. "Son, I have a really bad feeling about this."

"Me too, Eddie. Me too."

CHAPTER SIX

SAWYER ONLY HEARD ONE SIDE OF ROYCE'S CONVERSATION, BUT it was enough to know something was really wrong. SPD officers and sheriff's deputies were at their lawyer's office? Acid churned in his gut, and a paralyzing fear gripped his heart as Royce wrapped things up. What the hell had happened? And how would it affect their adoption or even their ability to take Darla home? He felt an emotional tsunami building and willed himself to calm down. He probably could've talked himself off the ledge with his normal processes if not for his exhaustion. Sawyer's brain didn't want to settle down and be reasonable; it wanted to throw a fucking tantrum.

"Okay," Royce told Eddie. "I'll see you soon."

A warm hand landed between Sawyer's shoulder blades, and his mother's comforting scent calmed his surging turmoil. "I promise that everything is going to be okay." And even though she couldn't possibly make those guarantees, Sawyer believed her.

He tilted his head to rest against hers. "I need to do something, but I can't seem to move."

Royce came to stand in front of him. "Will you call Charlie and ask him what's going on? There are SPD cruisers on the scene, but it seems like CCSD is in charge. That means the law office isn't the primary scene for whatever happened."

The simple suggestion snapped Sawyer out of his fugue. He glanced at the bassinet where their daughter slept peacefully and mustered the energy to pull his shit together. Charlie Price, his former partner and now the county undersheriff, would know what was going on. "That's a great idea. I'll call him now." Sawyer retrieved his phone and scrolled through his contacts.

Royce walked to the bassinet and stroked Darla's soft cheek. "There's nothing for you to worry about, sweetheart. Not about the tongue tie procedure or whatever is happening at the lawyer's office. Your daddies will make everything right."

Christ, had Royce just lied to their daughter six hours into parenting? Sawyer knew the message was more for the adults in the room than the sleeping infant, but Darla wriggled in her little cocoon and made the cutest baby sigh he'd ever heard.

"Aww," the grandmothers collectively said as they moved toward the bassinet.

Sawyer pulled up Charlie's contact info and tapped the call icon before lifting the phone to his ear. He wasn't surprised when his call went to voicemail after several rings. "Charlie," he said. "It's Sawyer. I've got a time-sensitive situation going on and need your help. Our daughter was born this morning. We can't take her home from the hospital without our attorney filing legal documents with the court, but all attempts to reach her have been unsuccessful. My father-in-law rode over to the law office to see why no one had returned our calls. He said the place is swarming with CCSD officers. I'm not feeling very good about this. Can you please call me as soon as possible and let me know what's going on? Talk soon." He returned the phone to his pocket with a frustrated sigh. "Now what?"

"Well," Jo said. "I'm going to the waiting room to meet Eddie when he returns. I'll send Barron back to meet his granddaughter." She hugged everyone goodbye, gave one last longing look at Darla, and headed out.

Royce crossed the room and flopped down on the sofa as if his legs wouldn't support him any longer. "This would be easier to handle if we'd managed more than a few hours of sleep last night."

Evangeline snorted, then covered her mouth to hide her grin. "Sorry. But...get used to it. Nothing will ever be the same. Not sleep. Not sex. Nothing." She looked wistfully at the sleeping baby. "And you won't regret a single thing. You'll learn how to function with less of... everything."

Royce leaned forward, placed his elbows on his knees, and hung his head. "I feel cheated." His voice was low, gruff, and raw from the emotions he'd kept in check up to that point. "We've been dreaming and planning for Darla much longer than nine months. And yeah, I expected to feel a little fear today, but I figured it would be the same worries all parents have, not this gut-wrenching turmoil that our dreams are teetering on the edge of disaster." Royce raised his head and met Sawyer's gaze. "I won't give you sh...crap about needing to be in charge anymore."

Sawyer chuckled for the first time in what felt like forever. "I won't hold my breath."

"Seriously," Royce said. "You're only a control freak because you can do things better than nearly everyone else."

Grimacing, Sawyer replied, "Baby, I don't think that's the compliment you thought it would be."

Royce growled his frustration and rubbed his eyes. "I hate that we have to rely on a judge to decide that we're a legitimate family. It's unfair. And I just feel…"

"Vulnerable," Sawyer suggested as he sat beside his husband. He raised his hand to rub Royce's upper back.

"Yes." The word came out in a tortured hiss as he leaned into Sawyer's touch. "I don't enjoy feeling this way."

"Me either, and yes, I try to avoid feeling helpless as often as I can. But we aren't in control, and we need to trust that the universe will make things right for us." Sawyer leaned forward and kissed Royce's shoulder. "We're going to give ourselves about five minutes to sulk and mentally throw our tantrums, and then we're going to take action."

"Like what?" Royce asked. "We can't leave our daughter alone here and storm the crime scene to demand answers."

"Shhh." Sawyer dug his fingers into Royce's scalp the way he liked. "We have four minutes."

Royce huffed out a heavy sigh. "Fine."

Sawyer closed his eyes and let his riotous emotions flood in and slosh around. There was the fear and frustration Royce described, but there was the absolute joy he'd felt during Darla's delivery and holding her against his bare chest. They would find a way through this like they did everything in life—together.

"Okay." Royce's assertive voice penetrated through Sawyer's meditative peace. "There are still two more minutes on the clock, but I'm done moping."

Sawyer opened his eyes to find his mother had snatched Darla out of her bassinet. She was sitting in the glider with her feet propped up on the matching stool. Evangeline wore the most serene expression on her face as she cooed softly to Darla. He looped his arms around Royce's shoulders and pulled him close. "We won't be fighting this alone." He nodded in his mother's direction. "If someone tries to screw us over and take our girl, they'll have to go through my mother first."

Evangeline looked in their direction, a devious smile curving her lips. "And Eddie."

"The superhero duo no one ever would've predicted," Royce replied.

Sawyer chuckled. "Yet, it's the team everyone probably needs."

There was a brief knock at the door before Barron opened it and entered the room. "Congratulations, guys." His gaze shifted to the corner of the room, and his face lit up with joy when he spotted his wife and new granddaughter. "You are going to share her, right?" Barron asked as he crossed the room to the sink.

"Maybe." But Evangeline stood up slowly once he washed his hands and gestured for Barron to take the chair. Then she carefully transferred the sleeping baby to his arms.

"The grandpa gig never gets old," Barron said. "Hello, beautiful angel."

Evangeline sat on the footstool, and the two of them fussed over the newest member of the family. Sawyer and Royce watched them for a few minutes before they turned their attention back to one another.

"We're not without resources," Sawyer whispered. "Our chief is married to the sheriff. We'd never tap into that connection without there being a valid reason, and they know it."

"True." Royce opened the internet browser on his phone and started typing in the search bar. He hit Enter and sucked in a breath at the results he found.

Sawyer's stomach knotted painfully at the sound, but he leaned closer to see what caused the reaction. There was a headline about an early morning hit-and-run involving a jogger in Chatham County. Beneath that, in smaller print, it read: *Prominent attorney left dead in the road. Was this accidental or intentional?* "Click the link," Sawyer said.

Royce's thumb shook as he tapped his phone to open the article. The text was brief, as the reporter claimed that law enforcement hadn't revealed many details. She led with the time and location of the accident before she got to the person's identity. "Ned Owens. Isn't he a founding partner at Ivy's firm?"

"Yes," Sawyer said, remembering the encounter between Ivy and Ned the previous…night? Had that just occurred yesterday? "He'd wanted to talk to Ivy about something but hadn't wanted to keep us waiting."

"I wonder if the source of his concern is the same reason he's dead," Royce said, then shook his head. "That's a big leap. This is real life, not a movie or TV show. His death is likely the result of a tragic accident."

"Maybe," Sawyer said. "But Ned Owens looked deeply troubled last night."

"You only observed him for a few minutes," Royce countered.

"It was long enough to know something had really shaken him. And with the police presence at the office…" Sawyer tapped his chest where his heart lay beating inside. "Something bad was going on, and now we're caught in the middle of it."

"I like my conclusion much better," Royce said, but Sawyer could tell his opinion was wavering. When Royce whispered, "Shit," Sawyer knew his husband had also pitched a tent in the conspiracy theory camp. "Now what?"

"We reach out to every resource in our arsenal," Sawyer replied, then began listing them off. "Mendoza, Abe, and Charlie. Hell, even Commissioner Rigby would go out of her way to help us."

Nodding, Royce said, "And don't forget Felix. That guy always knows what's going on."

Someone knocked twice on the door, and Kitty poked her head inside. "I'm sorry to bother you, but there's an Ivy Reeves here to see you guys. She's claiming to be your family attorney."

"Thank goodness," Royce said.

Relief washed over Sawyer and infused him with a burst of energy. "She is our attorney. We've been trying to get in touch with her all day. Please send her back."

Kitty glanced to the corner of the room where the grandparents were canoodling with Darla. The nurse grimaced when she met Sawyer's gaze again. "I wish I could make an exception to our visitor rules, but we don't allow more than four people in the room. Other than the baby, that is."

"It's no problem," Evangeline said. "Dad and I will duck out and make dinner arrangements for you guys while you talk to Ivy. How does the Hummingbird Café sound?"

Sawyer's stomach growled its approval. "Perfect."

Evangeline stood up and eased Darla from Barron's arms. She crossed the room and carefully placed her in the bassinet. "I'll be back in a bit, sweetheart. Don't grow up too fast while I'm gone."

Barron smiled down at his granddaughter before placing his hand on Evangeline's lower back and guiding her from the room. "Text me later and let me know what you want to eat," he said.

"I know what they like," Evangeline replied. "Text us when we can come back and snuggle Darla."

When Kitty left to get Ivy, Sawyer stood up and paced the length of the room. "It's going to be okay. Whatever Owens was involved with or knew about won't affect us."

Royce crossed his arms over his chest and studied him. Exhaustion and stress tugged the corners of his mouth down into a slight frown. Sawyer missed his wicked grin and the way it lit up his eyes and dared Sawyer to kiss him. "Are you trying to convince yourself or me?"

Sawyer stopped in front of Royce and notched his chin higher. "I was talking to our daughter. She's nervous."

They both looked at the bassinet where Darla dreamed peacefully.

"Uh-huh," Royce said as he took Sawyer's hands in his. "You are right. It's going to be okay because the three of us will still have each other."

Sawyer nodded. "But this feels like a dream, right? We're going to wake up any minute, and Kelsey hasn't gone into labor yet, and our adoption doesn't hang in the balance."

Royce scowled at him. "There's only room for one doomsday alarmist, and I've claimed the role with my theatrics earlier."

"Fine, but I think we should get to take turns," Sawyer replied.

Ivy arrived before Royce could respond. She was barely recognizable in her current state. Instead of her usual business attire, she wore jeans and an oversized sweater. The only familiar thing about her was the briefcase she carried in her right hand. Ivy's long hair hung lank around her face, and her eyes and nose were red from crying. No wonder Kitty questioned whether this woman was their attorney.

"I'm incredibly sorry it's taken me so long to get back to you," she said. "I…I…" Fresh tears threatened, and Ivy turned her head to gather herself. Swallowing hard, their attorney straightened her shoulders and faced them once more. "This is so unprofessional, and I am so sorry. I'm just in shock."

"We heard about Ned Owens," Sawyer said. "We're very sorry for your loss."

Ivy cleared her throat and nodded. "Yes, thank you. It's been a horrific day. Started out good though," she said with a weak smile. "I got your message about Darla's early arrival, but I got the news about Ned before I could call you back."

"He was struck while jogging?" Royce asked.

Ivy sucked in a shaky breath and nodded. "And I don't think it was an accident." She shook her head. "No, that's not right." Ivy's eyes darkened with determination as she straightened her shoulders. "I know damn well it wasn't an accident."

The seasoned detective stirred inside Sawyer to take over for the exhausted new dad. His senses sharpened as his brain fog cleared. "Are you basing your opinion on something the investigators said to you or on the conversation you had with Ned last night?"

Ivy stiffened and narrowed her eyes. "How did you know about my discussion with Ned?"

"I overheard bits of your exchange with Ned outside the conference room," Sawyer said. "Ned seemed stressed and said that he needed to speak to you about a pressing matter. You offered to meet with him right then since Miguel hadn't yet arrived, but Ned said he'd call you later."

"Did he call you?" Royce pressed.

Ivy's shoulders slumped, but she maintained eye contact with them. "He did. And yes, based on our conversation last night and the interview questions from detectives this morning, I am convinced someone murdered Ned."

"And since CCSD is crawling all over your law office, I assume you shared what you could with investigators," Sawyer said.

"Of course," Ivy replied. "I want this lunatic brought to justice, and I don't want anyone else to get hurt."

Royce tilted his head to the right. "Do you think the rest of the lawyers and staff are targets?"

"Possibly, but we won't be the only ones hurt when the allegations come to light." Ivy looked down at the briefcase, then gestured to the small dinette set at the opposite end of the suite. "Let's sit down and talk. There are things I shouldn't tell you, but I feel like leaving you in the dark is unethical and just plain wrong."

Sawyer and Royce exchanged nervous glances before following Ivy. They sat opposite her and waited while she sorted through her briefcase. Was she using the search as a delay tactic? Sawyer was at his wit's end by the time she pulled their legal documents from the briefcase and set them on the table.

"I was so rattled by the news this morning that I left the house without my cell phone. I am truly sorry for the worry my lack of communication has caused you." She tapped the paperwork with her finger. "These are copies of the legal documents I filed in family court after I finished my police interviews."

"Does this mean we can take her home when she's discharged?" Sawyer asked.

"No, this is just the paperwork I filed on your behalf. It still needs to go before Judge Hampton for her signature, but I've been assured that won't be a problem. The family court is used to dealing with time-sensitive situations, and I am confident that you will receive your post-birth orders tomorrow morning. The clerk will send that directly to the hospital once the judge signs off on the custody agreement. I'll get a copy of the order, and I'll make sure you receive one as well." She pushed the documents forward, and Sawyer took them from her. Ivy laced her hands together and rested them on top of her briefcase. "I wish I could guarantee the rest of the process will go as smoothly as we've discussed, but I won't lie to you. Considering Ned's death and the allegations that will soon follow, I expect a delay before the court will finalize your adoption."

Sawyer's stomach sank so fast that the floor must've fallen out from under his chair. The world spun, and everything around him became a blur. Royce's warm hand landed on his thigh, and everything settled into focus once more.

"Allegations of wrongdoing by your firm?" Royce asked. A husky edginess had crept into his voice, making him sound more like Eddie.

"No," Ivy said adamantly. "I promise you that our law firm was not a willing participant in any of the alleged activities."

Her assurances didn't make Sawyer feel better. "What kind of alleged activities?"

"I'm not in a position to say right now." Ivy held up both hands. "I know that seems unfair, but there are oaths I've taken and the legal advice from our attorneys that I can't ignore. I am being as transparent with the police as I can legally be right now."

"Can you respond with a simple yes-or-no answer to one question?" Royce asked her.

Ivy pursed her lips in contemplation. "I can't agree to that without knowing what you want to ask."

"Okay, I'll ask my question, and you decide how you want to respond," Royce replied patiently. "Is our expected delay because of past adoptions or custody cases your firm has presented to the family court?"

Ivy's mouth popped open with a soft gasp. "How could you know that?"

"We're detectives," Royce reminded her. "We can smell bullshit a mile away, so I need you to cut to the chase and be a hundred percent honest with us. What are the chances that your firm has acted in a way that will cause the court to deny our petition for adoption?"

Just hearing the words spoken out loud made Sawyer sick. He pressed a hand to his stomach as if that gesture alone could make it settle.

Ivy's demeanor shifted into the fierce family law advocate they knew. "There's zero chance of that, guys. Our law firm has done nothing wrong. If there is fault to be found, it won't be with us." She held her hands up, palms out. "And that's all I can say."

Sawyer wanted to press her for more answers but knew it wouldn't do him any good. He released a frustrated breath and turned to face Royce. "The rest can wait as long as we get the post-birth order signed in time to leave the hospital."

Royce nodded and squeezed Sawyer's thigh. "Keep us posted?"

"Of course. I'm going to head home and retrieve my phone. I'll be in touch as soon as I hear from Judge Hampton's clerk." She pushed back from the table and stood up. "Congratulations. Please don't let any of this overshadow the joy of welcoming your baby girl into the world. I know it's hard to have faith, but everything is going to be okay."

She couldn't know that for certain, but Sawyer needed to believe it, even if he was setting himself up for future heartache. But she was right about one thing. All the fretting and worrying would only rob them of precious time with their little girl, and he didn't want to miss a single cute sigh or adorable expression Darla made.

Their family suite became a flurry of activity between the grandparents rotating in and out and the specialists' visits during the next two feeding cycles. Both the speech pathologist and the lactation consultant agreed with Dr. Edwards' assessment, and Darla's procedure was scheduled for seven thirty in the morning. Sawyer wanted to think they'd manage a little rest over the next twelve hours, but he wasn't betting on it. He would give it his best effort if he could kindly evict his mother and father from the suite without causing hurt feelings. Both sets of parents had fed them well, loved them up, and boosted their morale with encouragement. The support was absolutely wonderful, but Sawyer was ready for some quiet time with his husband and daughter. Eddie and Jo had taken the hint during their last rotation when Royce let out a jaw-cracking yawn, but Evangeline was too focused on her Darla to notice when he tried it with her. Sawyer's youngest nephew was ten, so it had been a very long time since one of her children had presented her with a newborn. She'd been willing to test the limits of the hospital visiting hours.

"Isn't she the most beautiful miracle you've ever seen?" Evangeline asked wistfully.

It wasn't the first time she'd asked, and it wouldn't be the last. Sawyer's answer would always be the same. "Yes." His phone vibrated with a text from Kelsey, asking if it would be okay to visit Darla. The timing couldn't have been better. Evangeline wouldn't refuse Kelsey time to visit with the miracle she'd helped to create. He typed out a quick reply to Kels and set his phone down. "Mom, Kelsey wants to spend time with Darla."

Evangeline didn't look away from the bassinet. "Barron doesn't mind going to the waiting room."

"Andrew is coming too," Sawyer said. "And then these new dads need to attempt some sleep."

His mother sighed deeply. "I know. I'm being awfully selfish." She placed a gentle hand on Darla's belly. "But I love her so much."

"Tomorrow morning is going to be really eventful with her procedure, recovery, and working with the specialists to get our girl on track. I think it would be best if we waited until midafternoon for visits. I'll keep you posted on everything that happens."

Evangeline turned to face him. "And you'll send pictures."

"Of course," Royce said.

She crossed the room and threw her arms around Sawyer's neck and then Royce's. "I love you both so much."

"And we love you," Sawyer told her. "Thank you for everything today. It's been an emotional roller coaster, and your support means everything to us."

"We're glad we could help," Barron said after hugging each of them. "Let us know if we can bring you anything when we come to-morrow afternoon."

Sawyer and Royce exhaled sighs of relief once they were alone. They reached for each other, stepping into a warm embrace that lingered until there was a soft knock on the door. Sawyer opened it, expecting to see Kelsey in a wheelchair, but she stood in the hallway, though slightly hunched. "Come in and sit down. I don't think gravity is your friend right now."

"I've been sitting or lying down all day. I needed to move my legs, and we're just two doors down." Kelsey shuffled inside with Andrew close behind her, ready to catch her if things went sideways.

"She's a stubborn woman," Andrew said with a smirk.

"They make the world go round," Sawyer told him.

Kelsey moved to the bassinet and smiled down at Darla. "How's she doing?"

They told Kels about Darla's upcoming procedure, and she made cooing noises as she stroked her cheek.

"Kids are resilient," Kelsey said. "She won't remember the discomfort or hold a grudge against you, especially once the milk starts flowing." She looked over at them and smiled. "Is fatherhood everything you dreamed it would be?"

Sawyer and Royce exchanged a loaded glance, both of them wondering what to say about the situation with their law firm. If Miguel had informed Kelsey, she would've brought it up already.

"What's that look about?" Kelsey said. "You guys just held an entire conversation in five seconds."

"It's been quite an eventful day with some unsettling developments," Sawyer said.

"Oh, this doesn't sound good." Kelsey shuffled to the glider and eased down into it. "Okay. I'm ready."

"Wait," Andrew said. He strode across the room and sat down on the sofa. "I'm ready too."

Sawyer and Royce relayed everything they knew up to that point, and as he suspected, Kelsey hadn't heard about Ned Owens' death. Her beautiful face betrayed the shock, sorrow, and anger she felt.

"I texted Miguel to let him know I had the baby, and he acknowledged my message without mentioning the situation with Ned."

"He might not have known then," Andrew said. "Even if he did, Miguel likely isn't privy to whatever Ivy knows. Their potential legal issues might not affect him."

"Doubtful," Kelsey replied. "If there's even a hint of unethical practices in a single adoption, all firms involved will be under scrutiny to see what they knew and when they knew it. I wouldn't be surprised if a judge reviews all their cases within a certain time frame." She shook her head in dismay. "I listened to a podcast about this recently. A judge in Michigan reviewed every single case a law firm handled for an adoption agency. Those adoptive families were terrified of having their babies taken away."

Sawyer died a thousand deaths before his next heartbeat. This was how it would end for him after years of trying to ensure a healthy cardiovascular system. His hand went to his chest automatically as he focused on breathing.

Andrew must've read his panic because he settled a hand on Kelsey's back. "My love, that kind of conjecture isn't helping anyone."

Kelsey looked over at Sawyer, and her eyes widened in alarm. "Oh, honey," she said. "I'm so sorry. I didn't mean to imply that this situation is the same." She tried to push up out of the glider, but Sawyer went to her instead and sat on the stool. Kelsey took his hands. "The judge in Michigan upheld every single adoption. No one is coming to rip your baby girl out of your life. I won't let that happen."

"No one will," Andrew said.

"And your friend Charlie from the sheriff's department hasn't responded to your message yet?" Kelsey asked.

"He sent a text a few hours ago letting me know he'd return my call as soon as he could. In all the excitement, I forgot that Mendoza and Abe are out of town. That means Charlie is acting sheriff, and he's likely got his hands full with this investigation."

"Let me know what you find out."

"Of course," Sawyer said.

Kelsey reached for his hand. "Everything is going to be okay."

Darla let out a soft little whimper in her bassinet, and he launched to his feet.

"See, little miss agrees with me," Kelsey said. "Now, help me up so I can see her."

"I'll bring her to you," Sawyer replied.

Kelsey settled back in the glider and propped her feet up on the vacated stool. "If you insist."

Darla blinked her eyes when he approached, and he swore she locked her gaze on him, even if only for a few seconds.

"There's my girl," he whispered as he lifted her from the bassinet. "Someone special wants to snuggle with you for a bit."

Kelsey held her arms straight out in front of her and wiggled her fingers in a give-me gesture. Sawyer transferred Darla over and smiled as Kelsey studied the miracle she created and carried for them. "My heart is so full," she told the baby. "What a blessing to be part of your life and watch you grow. I get to suffuse you with my love and then go home and sleep peacefully through the night."

The guys all chuckled, but there wasn't a dry eye in the room.

Kelsey peeled the hat back a little to see her hair. "Ella had beautiful black hair like this. Curls for days." She looked up and smiled. "I'm surprised Evangeline hasn't adorned her locks yet."

"She didn't want her head to get cold, but she's already picked out a headband for her birth announcement photos," Sawyer said.

Darla yawned big and triggered a domino effect around the room.

"That's our cue to leave," Kelsey told Andrew. "Everyone needs their rest."

Sawyer took Darla from Kelsey, and Andrew helped her stand.

"Don't even think about offering to get a wheelchair," Kelsey told her husband.

"Wouldn't dream of it," Andrew replied with a wink at Sawyer.

They promised to stop by again before Kelsey got discharged and shuffled out the door. Sawyer checked the feeding schedule and saw they were only thirty minutes from their next attempt. He decided to snuggle Darla until then, so he eased down to the sofa so Royce could join him. It was funny how still his husband could be when it came time to admire the littlest Locke.

Sawyer's phone vibrated on the table with an incoming call, and his pulse kicked up a notch when he saw the caller ID. "It's Charlie. Can you grab that?"

Royce stretched forward and answered the call, switching to speakerphone. "Thanks for getting back to us," he said.

"Sorry it took me so long, guys. This one is…complicated."

"No chance it was an accidental hit-and-run?" Sawyer asked.

"Oh, hell no," Charlie replied. "Do you remember the famous case from years ago where the wife ran over her husband in a hotel parking lot after she caught him cheating, and then circled the building to hit him again and again?"

Nausea rose swiftly, and Sawyer thought he was going to be sick.

"Christ," Royce said. "It was that bad?"

"Let's just say Ned Owens' killer made sure he was dead." Charlie's exhaustion was evident in the heavy sigh that followed. "You know how complicated homicide cases are when the victim is an attorney and the suspect is likely one of their clients. There's all that privileged information shit to contend with."

Sawyer sat taller. "So you have a suspect in mind already?"

"Yeah. The partners and associates at Owens' firm are cooperating as much as they can without committing ethics violations, but our primary suspect has a solid alibi."

"They've enlisted help," Sawyer said. "Someone close that they can rely on."

"And we're leaving no stone unturned. I promise. Congratulations, by the way," Charlie said. "I can't believe I didn't lead with that. I'm such an asshole."

Sawyer chuckled. "No, you've got a lot on your plate right now. I hate to press you, but is there any information you can share with us? Our attorney has informed us that our adoption process will probably get delayed because of Ned Owens' death and the dire allegations that might go public. I just want to know what we're dealing with."

"For anyone else, the answer would be hell no. This is going to be a high-profile case, and my professional reputation is at stake, but I know you'd have my back if the situation were reversed."

"Hell yes, I would," Sawyer said. "This stays between the three of us. Well, four if you count Darla, but she's sound asleep, and her communication skills are limited."

Charlie chuckled. "Fair enough. Here's what I know so far. A young lady recently reached out to Ned Owens and alleged that she hadn't wanted to give up her baby for adoption. She claimed she was coerced."

"How is that possible?" Sawyer asked. "Didn't she hire his agency to assist her?"

"Not exactly," Charlie said. "There's a local agency that connects prospective families with pregnant mothers who've chosen to place their babies for adoption. The mother gets to meet the parents and choose who gets to adopt their baby. The adoptive parents pay a steep sum to cover all the legal fees plus the mother's healthcare expenses during pregnancy and recovery. They pay for housing, clothing, and food, depending on the expectant mother's circumstances and needs, so the amounts are never the same. The agency is supposed to retain a fee for its services."

"And this agency hired our law firm to oversee the adoptions?" Royce asked.

"Affirmative."

"A fucking baby broker?" Sawyer snarled. "I can't believe it."

"Baby brokers are illegal in Georgia," Charlie replied in a slow, feminine drawl. "This woman runs a bona fide adoption agency."

"Why do I get the feeling you're quoting her?" Sawyer asked.

Charlie snorted. "Because you know me very well, partner. The whistleblower also claimed that Miss Bona Fide kept most of the money owed to her, and she claims there are others who are willing to testify to the same coercion and neglect."

Royce and Sawyer looked at one another and mouthed, "Fuck."

"It's a mess," Charlie agreed. "Ned has been in touch with Miss Bona Fide, who allegedly threatened him. I can't verify the claim until I get a judge to approve warrants for records, but that's always hard sorting through what's privileged and fair game. Like I said, I'll keep you posted as I learn things. I hope this doesn't make things harder for you guys."

"Same," Royce said. "Thanks, Charlie."

"No problem. You guys get rest when you can. Parenthood is a marathon, not a sprint."

They exchanged goodbyes and disconnected. Royce returned the phone to the table, and they sat in stunned silence as they watched their baby girl sleep. Sawyer couldn't resist pulling her closer and placing a gentle kiss against her knitted cap.

"Your daddies love you so much, Pumpkin," he told her. "We will make this right."

CHAPTER SEVEN

ROYCE SMILED DOWN AT DARLA, WHO DOZED PEACEFULLY IN his arms. It was time for her first feeding after the frenectomy, and she didn't look remotely interested in doing anything but sleep. Unfortunately, that wasn't an option for her. They had quite an audience in the room to observe the feeding and give pointers if Darla still struggled to latch on. If she did well with her next few bottles, they'd discharge her to go home instead of spending another night at the hospital. Royce and Sawyer were eager to take their daughter home and settle into their new routine. But no pressure. They obviously wanted what was best for Darla more than their own comfort. "Dr. Edwards must've given you the good stuff, Lil Pumpkin?" Royce teased. "You're zonked out." Her little eyelashes fluttered, but she didn't open her eyes.

Bailey, the lactation consultant, stood at his right shoulder, and Chelsea, the speech pathologist, stood to his left. They both laughed while Sawyer offered him an encouraging wink.

Royce brushed the bottle's nipple across Darla's bottom lip. "Come on, sweetheart. I know you're sleepy, but you need to drink your formula so you can grow big and strong."

Darla arched her back and stretched her arms. Royce brushed the nipple across her lips again, and this time, she turned her head to pursue it.

"That's good," Bailey said. "She's reacting to the stimulus, and her feeding instincts are kicking in. Keep doing that."

On the next swipe, Darla opened her mouth and latched on, tentatively at first, as if she remembered the discomfort from previous attempts.

"Attagirl," Royce whispered. Darla opened her eyes and looked up at him. "There's my hungry princess." Her eyelids fluttered closed again, but she continued drinking her formula at an easy pace.

Bailey and Chelsea observed, offering tips and pointing out cues that indicated Darla might need a break. Royce stopped after an ounce to burp her, and then Sawyer took over the hot seat and continued her feeding. Bailey suggested they try out a different feeding position to see what felt most comfortable to him and to gauge Darla's response. Sawyer had never looked more serene than at that moment, and Royce couldn't resist snapping his hundredth picture of the day. He didn't even care that fawning ladies surrounded his husband. When Darla opened her eyes and looked up at Sawyer, Royce repositioned himself to capture the image. Sawyer smiled down at the baby girl he'd longed for as she gazed up at him. Their eye contact lasted only a few seconds, but the memory would endure for a lifetime.

Sawyer snapped his gaze up to meet Royce's. "I think she likes me."

"She's crazy about you." As grateful as he was for their help, Royce wanted to shoo Bailey and Chelsea out of the room so they could share these intimate moments as a family of three.

Maybe Bailey picked up on his thoughts, because she looked over at Chelsea and said, "I think they've got this under control." To Royce, she added, "When you're done with the bottle, just set it aside so I can document her progress when I return. I'll let you guys handle the next feeding on your own and will return for the one after that for my final assessment. Do you guys have questions for either of us?"

"I'm good," Royce said. "How about you?"

"I don't have questions right now," Sawyer said. "If something occurs to me, I'll write it down for when you come back later."

"Sounds good," Chelsea said. "You have our numbers, so please call if you need anything. We're here to help."

"And we appreciate you both," Sawyer said.

Royce curled up on the edge of the sofa nearest the glider and watched Darla's tiny mouth move as she took in her nourishment. "What a difference a day makes," he said. "Yesterday, she didn't want to take a bottle, and we feared we wouldn't be able to take her home from the hospital. We've got a signed custody order, and our Lil Pumpkin is drinking like a pro."

"I was thinking the same thing, but my time reference was even smaller," Sawyer said. "Just a few hours ago, Kelsey had to sign the paperwork to authorize Darla's procedure because the post-birth agreement hadn't arrived in time. The precariousness of our situation really struck home then. I'm trying not to fixate on just how tenuous our rights are. What if…" Sawyer's voice trailed off, and he shook his head. "Nope. I am not fixating on that right now. The situation with our law firm is very stressful, but Ivy hasn't led us astray. She told us the judge overseeing our adoption is fair and LGBTQ+ friendly."

Darla had conked out again, and her tiny mouth had stopped moving. Sawyer eased the bottle free and set it on the table. He took the spit rag he'd slung over his shoulder and dabbed at the formula at the corners of her mouth. Then he arranged Darla against his chest and alternated between pats and rubs to burp her.

"We're taking this sweet girl home with us, and we'll complete the requirements to make her adoption official," Sawyer said. "Those are the things we can control." Darla let out a tiny burp, and Sawyer's face lit up with absolute joy. "I got her to burp!"

"Nice job, Dad," Royce said.

"Wasn't that the cutest little sound you ever heard?" Darla scrunched up her body, and she grunted a little as air came out the other end. "And I got her to fart!"

Royce leaned back and laughed. "Those are going to get bigger and less cute, and so will her poopy diapers."

"Doesn't scare me," Sawyer said as he joined Royce on the sofa. Darla made a little whiny sound, and Sawyer soothed her by rubbing gentle circles on her back. Father and daughter snuggled closer to him, with Sawyer resting his head against Royce's shoulder. "I live with you, after all."

The tone of their conversation went downhill fast, but it felt so good to talk about stupid, random things while snuggling their daughter instead of fretting about an uncertain future.

"Knock, knock," Kelsey said from the open doorway. Andrew stood behind her wheelchair with two large bags slung over each shoulder. "Is it okay if I say goodbye before we head out?"

Royce looked up from feeding Darla. "Of course. Come in. How are you feeling?"

Kelsey held out her hand and rocked it from side to side. "Like I just squeezed a baby out of my cute vagina," she replied as Andrew wheeled her into the room. "But mostly, I'm homesick and miss my Ella Bella Bean." Kelsey looked around the room and noted Sawyer's absence with a raised brow.

"He's getting antsy," Royce said with a chuckle. "He packed up everything we're not using and took it down to the car to prepare for our discharge later today."

Kelsey leaned forward and smiled at Darla. "Aww, look at her go. She's doing so well now. Looks like the procedure was a triumph."

"It was," Royce said. "Thank you for stepping in." Emotion welled up suddenly, and tears filled his eyes. "It's not the first time you've stepped up when we've needed you most."

"And it won't be the last." Kelsey's gaze shimmered with unshed tears too, and she used the corner of her hot pink cardigan to dab at her eyes. "Dang you, Royce Locke."

Sawyer entered the room with a smirk. "I say that a lot, but with more forceful language." He looked at their daughter and added, "Well, at least I used to. It'll be dang you from now on." He leaned down and kissed the top of Kelsey's head. "Are we crying happy tears, or has something happened?" Sawyer looked at Andrew. "Should we get emotional too?"

"I'm trying to thank Kelsey for our daughter, so yes." Royce looked up at Andrew and grimaced. "And thank you for your sacrifice also."

Andrew chuckled and waved him off. "Don't worry about me."

"Only some parts of me are off-limits," Kelsey said with a wink. "And I won't have late-night feedings and loss of sleep to contend with. My guy will be just fine."

"Babe," Andrew said with a grimace. Heat climbed his neck and turned his cheeks pink. "The guys don't want to hear this."

Royce bit his bottom lip to keep from laughing because he was pretty certain that Sawyer and Kelsey shared many things their spouses wouldn't like. "Do you want to hold her before you leave?"

Kelsey's expression grew wistful, but she shook her head. "Let her drink her bottle in peace." She reached out and caressed Darla's tiny fist. "I was hoping to catch Evangeline too. She stopped by with a lovely gift this morning, but I was napping. I'd hoped to thank her in person, but I will call her instead."

"You just missed her," Sawyer said. "She's at our house making sure things are ready for Darla's homecoming."

Kelsey laughed and smiled at him. "They've been ready for a while."

Sawyer shrugged. "You can see where I get some of my most neurotic tendencies. She's also making sure we have something delicious to eat tonight, so I'm not going to be mad about her fussing."

"When are the rest of your families coming to meet Darla?" Kelsey asked.

"Present company excluded, we're implementing a 'grandparents only' rule for the first week," Sawyer said. "And we're even limiting those visits until we figure out a routine."

"Uh-huh," Kelsey said. "Which one of you is going to tell Evangeline that it isn't a good time for her to see her granddaughter?"

Royce and Sawyer pointed at one another, and then they all laughed. Darla flinched slightly, cracked open one eye, but didn't cry or stop drinking.

Holding her stomach, Kelsey looked over her shoulder at Andrew. "On that note, it's time for us to leave."

"We have to flag down a nurse because I can't be trusted to wheel you out the doors," Andrew said.

"It's policy," Kelsey replied. "Don't get salty about it. You can bring the car around."

Andrew grumbled something unintelligible about policies while

Kelsey exchanged tearful goodbyes with Royce and Sawyer. They promised to send her pictures every day, and she vowed to get them hooked on reality television during their paternity leave.

"Not going to happen," Royce called out.

Kelsey's devilish cackle echoed in the hallway, and Darla wriggled in response.

"That's a sound she's used to hearing," Royce said.

"Maybe we should get Kelsey to record herself reading books and play it for Darla if she gets fussy."

Royce reached over and smoothed out the adorable furrow in Sawyer's brow. "Don't worry that we're traumatizing our daughter by separating her from Kelsey, or fret that she doesn't like the sound of our voices."

"I wasn't," Sawyer protested weakly. But then he held up his thumb and forefinger an inch apart. "Perhaps a little. It's like I'm afraid to be happy."

"You're projecting the angst from issues you refuse to dwell on to the things you can fix. You're a problem solver."

Sawyer cringed, and his cheeks turned pink. "I sound fun."

"You're a fu…flipping delight."

"Nice catch," Sawyer said.

"No, you are."

Kitty walked into the room with paperwork in her hands. "I have your discharge papers."

"Yes!" Royce fist-pumped the air. "No offense. You've all been lovely."

"No, I get it," Kitty said. "You're looking forward to being comfortable in your own home." She looked around the room. "Wow, you're all packed up and ready to go. We just need to transfer Miss Darla Grace into her car seat so I can make sure she's strapped in properly. Then one of you will ride down in the wheelchair with her on your lap, while the other drives the car around to the porte cochère. I'll make sure her car seat snaps into the base correctly and turn you loose."

"I'll take the wheelchair, and you get the car," Sawyer said. "He's a big fan of the wheelchair scene in *Days of Thunder*. I can't imagine him challenging someone to a race with Darla on his lap, but let's not risk it."

Kitty laughed. "That's one of my grandpa's favorite movies, and I love that scene."

Sawyer looked at Royce and mouthed, "Grandpa," at him.

Royce barely resisted the urge to flip him off. He collected the paperwork from Kitty instead and looped Darla's diaper bag over his shoulder. This was his life now, carting around stuff to wipe butts and feed a little person, and he couldn't be happier. Royce practically levitated down the corridors and out to their SUV. Sawyer, Darla, and Kitty waited just inside the hospital until he pulled up under the canopy. Royce parked and walked around to the rear passenger side, where they'd installed the car seat base. He couldn't help but smile at the memory of Sawyer whipping out a small level to make sure they'd evenly secured it on both sides. He took full credit for that maneuver. Sawyer was pure Locke in name and attitude.

"Do you want me to snap in her carrier?" Royce asked Kitty.

"Not yet. I need to check the base's installation first."

Royce stepped out of the way as she performed her safety inspection.

"Snug as a bug," Kitty declared once she finished. "Excellent job."

Royce resisted the urge to preen, but just barely. He took the carrier from Sawyer and locked it into the base with a snap. He stepped aside again so Kitty could check the fit. She peeled back the light blanket Sawyer had draped over the car seat to keep Darla warm.

"You're good to go, guys," Kitty said. "It was lovely working with you both."

They thanked Kitty and climbed into the SUV—Royce behind the wheel and Sawyer in the back seat next to Darla. Royce cued the *Baby Mozart* soundtrack and eased away from the curb. One of the favorite baby gadgets he'd purchased was a car seat monitoring system for both vehicles. He mounted the camera at the rear of the vehicle and the display console on the dashboard. It would come in handy when they had to take Darla places by themselves, but he especially loved the feature during their first ride home. Royce glanced at the monitor every time he stopped at an intersection and fell deeper in love with both his husband and daughter. If only he could stop time and savor this moment longer. Then someone honked obnoxiously behind him when he'd remained stopped for an entire two seconds after a traffic light turned green.

"Jackass," Royce muttered under his breath.

"We heard that," Sawyer teased. "Pretty sure Darla's little bow mouth started to form the word already."

Royce chuckled and drove a few miles under the speed limit just to annoy the jerk behind him. They made it home without incident, though he'd irritated plenty of people by obeying the speed limits and traffic laws.

"We're home," Sawyer told Darla. "Bones and Dolly will be so excited to meet you."

"Doubt it," Royce replied. "Bones shares his dads with the dog he rescued, but I'm not sure what he'll think about a baby."

"Guess we're about to find out," Sawyer said as they pulled into the garage.

Royce cut the engine and pushed the button to close the door. "You get the baby, and I'll bring in the bags."

"We'll both take our baby inside, and we'll worry about the bags later."

Royce grabbed the diaper bag from the front seat and followed Sawyer around the vehicle so they could get Darla. She was sound asleep in her car seat and didn't react when they carried her inside the house. Royce sure did because something smelled delicious. He stopped in the kitchen, tilted his head back, and sniffed the air. "I smell beef and rich gravy."

"You could just open the lids on the pots and see what she made," Sawyer said.

"Where's the challenge in that?" Royce took another sniff. "I smell potatoes and carrots."

"No one smells carrots," Sawyer replied.

"I do."

Evangeline hustled into the kitchen, halted five feet away from them, and performed a happy dance. She took a deep breath and pushed her hands down as she exhaled. "Okay. I'm good." Evangeline calmly walked toward them and said, "Welcome home."

Sawyer kissed her cheek and gave her a one-armed hug. Royce wrapped her up with both arms when it was his turn.

"Dad is in the living room. He's taken over your recliner and your pets," Evangeline teased. "Eddie and Jo are on their way too. I hope you don't mind that I invited them."

"Of course not," Royce said.

Evangeline pressed her hands to her chest. "Phew. I just made so much food. There's no way you boys could eat all the leftovers."

"A challenge I would've happily accepted."

"What did you make?" Sawyer asked. "Royce smelled beef and a rich gravy, potatoes, and carrots. My vote is pot roast."

"Not this time," Evangeline said. "I made my beef and noodles, mashed potatoes, and glazed carrots. Jo is bringing pineapple up-side-down cake and a loaf of sourdough bread."

"Sounds like heaven," Sawyer said.

Evangeline winked. "It will taste like it too."

The little posse moved into the living room, where Barron indeed had taken over the recliner and had both pets in his lap. Dolly stood up and wagged her tail excitedly when she saw them, but Bones only cracked open one eye. Royce could hear him purring from across the room and suspected it would take more than a little stranger to dis-rupt his nap. Dolly moved to jump down, but Barron snagged her and placed her onto the floor. She darted over to them, looking at the car seat carrier with enormous eyes.

She barked twice and woke the baby from her nap. Darla blinked twice, scrunched up her face, and tested out her lung capacity. Dolly darted behind the recliner with her tail tucked between her legs. Sawyer set the carrier on the coffee table and unbuckled the crying baby while Royce tried to coax Dolly out from behind the chair. The small dog peeked her head around the corner, and Royce squatted down and patted the floor in front of him.

"It's okay, sweetheart," he cooed. "You didn't mean to scare the baby."

Dolly inched forward a few steps at a time, darting glances be-tween Royce and Sawyer, who sat on the couch with Darla. The baby had stopped crying, but she continued to fuss.

"I think she's looking for her next meal," Evangeline said when Darla nuzzled her face against Sawyer's chest.

"You won't find anything there, Pumpkin," Sawyer said.

"Want me to get a bottle ready?" Evangeline asked.

Sawyer checked his watch. "She's still got another hour before her next bottle. Let's see if we can get her a little closer."

Royce returned his attention to comforting Dolly. She ducked her head and ran to him, and Royce scooped her up and kissed the top of her head. "Let's go meet your human sister." He carried her over to the couch and sat down beside Sawyer and Darla. "You might not know it yet, but the two of you will be best friends someday." He looked over at the recliner, where Bones slept without a care. "It might take the cat a while to acknowledge Darla's existence, but he's going to love her too."

"I could do this all day, every day," Sawyer said, tipping his chin to Darla. "But I promised to help get the bags inside."

"Sounds like a mission for me," Barron said.

He powered the footrest down and stood up with Bones in his arms. The massive feline looked mad as hell when Barron set him back down in the chair alone. Bones looked at them on the couch, his gaze fixed on the wriggling baby against Sawyer's chest. The cat stood up, stretched his enormous body, and pranced across the end table between the two pieces of furniture and stalked toward them.

"Hi, Bonesy. I missed you." Sawyer extended a hand toward him, and Bones butted his head against it and purred loudly.

The feline got close enough to sniff Darla's leg. Dolly barked, the baby cried, and Bones got the hell out of there, heading down the hallway toward the bedrooms.

"Shhh, sweetheart," Sawyer said. "Dolly isn't nearly as mean as she sounds."

"She'll get used to the noise," Evangeline said.

The doorbell rang, the dog barked, the baby cried, and the cat stayed hidden.

"But will we?" Royce asked Sawyer.

"That will be Eddie and Jo," Evangeline said. "I'll get the door."

Royce stood up with Dolly. "I'll calm the dog."

"And I'll soothe the baby," Sawyer said. "We've got this."

And they found a harmonious balance over the next ninety minutes. They ate a fabulous meal and fussed over the world's most perfect baby girl as she mostly slept, reveling in the newfound happiness they'd found. Eventually, their company went home, the pets went to sleep, and Royce and Sawyer were alone with Darla.

"Let's transfer her to the bassinet in our bedroom and see if we can get some rest," Royce suggested. "We can worry about unpacking tomorrow."

"Everyone has advised us to rest when she does," Sawyer said. "I feel too amped up to sleep, but let's try."

Darla slept through the transfer and didn't stir while they took turns showering and brushing their teeth. She slept through them turning down the bed, shutting off the lights, and slipping between the sheets. Royce spooned up behind Sawyer, wrapped his hand around his waist, and kissed the back of his neck.

Sawyer wiggled closer and said, "Good night, love."

"Night."

Royce closed his eyes and sighed with contentment. He was just about to fall asleep when Darla cried, Dolly barked, and Bones darted out from under the bed and fled the room like his tail was on fire. Sawyer shook with laughter, and Royce rolled onto his back, grinning in the dark like a lunatic. "Home sweet home," he said.

CHAPTER EIGHT

Sawyer checked to make sure Darla was safely snug in her carrier. He slipped two fingers under the harness and decided for the third time in five minutes that she was perfectly secure. "Are you almost ready? I don't want to be late for her first pediatrician appointment," he called out.

Darla scrunched up her face at his slightly elevated voice, but she didn't cry, Dolly didn't bark, and Bones maintained his sentinel position on the arm of the sofa instead of running from the room. *Whew!* They were making progress. Their life had become chaotic, to say the least, since bringing Darla home from the hospital three days earlier, but Sawyer had never been happier.

"Hey," Royce said as he rushed into the living room. "No one cried or barked. I think we've managed a full twenty-four hours of relative peace without our littlest love reacting to Dolly's bark or setting it off." Royce's hair was still damp from his quick shower, and his sweatshirt was on backward. One sock was navy blue, and the other was black. The smudges of exhaustion under his eyes were a hue somewhere between the two and matched the set under Sawyer's eyes. Parenting wasn't for the weak. "And we won't be late. The doctor's office is only fifteen minutes away, and our appointment isn't for another hour."

"But there's going to be paperwork to complete," Sawyer said.

Royce shook his head. "I already completed the patient intake forms."

"When?"

"About two o'clock this morning, when Lil Pumpkin didn't want to go back to bed after her bottle. You'd crashed in the recliner, so I let you sleep. The doctor's office had sent a text with a link to their patient portal. I uploaded photos of my driver's license and insurance card, and I scanned our custody agreement for their records. Oh, and I set up her MyChart account too. The usernames and passwords for both are in our shared iPhone notes."

Sawyer stared at his husband as if seeing him for the first time. "Wow, I'm impressed."

"See," Royce said. "I've got everything under control."

Sawyer wiggled his index finger in Royce's direction. "Your sweatshirt is on backward, and your socks don't match."

Royce stopped mid-stride and looked down at his torso. "Huh. Well, I have most things under control." He pulled his arms free and repositioned his sweatshirt. Then he looked down at his feet. "These are close enough. No one will notice once I have shoes on." That was true enough. Royce sat down beside him and reached for his shoes under the coffee table, where Darla's car seat carrier rested. "She's sure sleeping well now. I think she's getting her days and nights mixed up."

"That's what the bags under our eyes say."

"No joke. Gave myself a fright when I looked in the mirror to shave this morning. I might have to use those under-eye thingies you keep in the refrigerator when we get home," Royce said.

"Oh yeah. I forgot about those. They have caffeine and vitamin C in them to brighten the skin under your eyes."

Royce snorted. "Sounds more like an adult Fruit Roll-Up than a beauty product."

Sawyer grimaced at the thought of trying to chew one of those things. Hard pass. "So, four or five under each eye should do the trick, right?"

"We might look more human and less zombie-like," Royce replied.

"I've been researching ways to help newborns develop healthy circadian rhythms so we can try to get Lil Miss on a better sleep schedule. I figured I'd run it by Dr. Edwards first. Maybe all newborns sleep during the day and stay awake at night. Could be she figures this out for herself."

"I'd rather get there sooner than later," Royce said. "We expected broken sleep, but I still imagined us having some semblance of a normal routine. Can you imagine trying to go to work like this? Yikes."

"No, I can't."

They were fortunate enough to have paid paternity leave for six weeks, and they both had weeks of accumulated sick pay and supplemental insurance that would kick in afterward. They'd been smart with their money and could enjoy three months off without financial worries. Other dads weren't as lucky and had to return to work right away. Sawyer vowed not to take their blessings for granted, but that didn't mean he wanted to keep Dracula's hours either.

Royce ran his hand over Bones' sleek back, but the cat didn't tear his eyes away from Darla. Their big boy always positioned himself where he could watch over her without getting too close. They figured it was only a matter of time before he took up guard duties immediately next to the baby. Dolly was more circumspect and a little jealous of the newest addition, but they were certain she'd come around too. Royce scooped the dog up from the floor to cradle her against his chest and kissed the top of her head. He ran a finger over the pink hair bow that declared Dolly was a big sister. "This is new."

"Evangeline bought it for her, and I put it on while you were sleeping this morning."

"Cute." Royce gave her one last kiss and set her on the sofa next to Bones. "Notice how neither of us is sleeping at the same time? I miss waking up next to you."

Sawyer leaned over and kissed him, his mouth lingering against warm lips. "It's only temporary." Darla made one of her cute little noises, pulling their attention to her. "And she's worth it." Sawyer checked his watch. "Let's load 'em up."

Royce stood up and lifted the carrier. "I've got Darla. You get the diaper bag." Sawyer reached for the large, dove-gray bag off the coffee table, but Royce stopped him. "That thing looks more like a mobile nursery. Surely, we don't need half the stuff you packed in there."

"You never know what's going to happen when you're out and about with a baby," Sawyer replied. "You need to be prepared for anything."

"Babe, we're coming right back. We're only going to be gone for ninety minutes, two hours tops."

"And in that time, Darla could spit up her formula and blow out a diaper. I put extra clothes in there for her. Plenty of diapers and wipes, plus butt cream in case she gets a rash. I have her little pre-mixed formula bottles and nipples in case the appointment runs into Darla's next feeding time. Oh, and I put snacks in there in case our blood sugar gets low since we're not eating on normal schedules."

"I'm not even sure when I ate last," Royce said.

"See." Sawyer tapped his temples. "I'm prepared for anything."

"Fine," Royce said, "but be sure to use your knees when lifting that hefty bag. We should probably invest in those weightlifting belts to stabilize our cores and support our spines."

A door on the far side of the waiting room opened, and a nurse dressed in Scooby-Doo scrubs stepped through it. She looked down at the tablet in her hand and said, "For Darla."

"That's us, kid," Royce said to their still-sleeping daughter. The chatter and activity in the busy pediatrician's office hadn't fazed her one bit. He stood up, and a rogue cashew nut fell to the floor.

Sawyer shook his head and picked it up off the carpet, dropping it in the trash can at the front of the room. Royce had eaten two single-serve packets of nuts and one of the apple cinnamon oatmeal bars. Then he'd gotten thirsty and downed a bottle and a half of water, all in the twenty minutes they'd had to wait to be seen. Sawyer made a mental note to pack more snacks and drinks next time.

"Hi, I'm Lily." The nurse smiled down at Darla. "She's so precious."

Lily fussed and cooed as she took some measurements. Their daughter only opened her eyes when the nurse removed her clothes to put her on the scale. She fussed in protest at the handling and lack of warmth.

"You can redress her now," Lily told them. "Her outfit is so cute."

"Thank you," Sawyer said.

They usually put her in comfy sleepers, but Sawyer dressed her in one of the adorable outfits they received at their baby shower. Tara and Candi had bought the ivory corduroy pants, long-sleeved onesie, and knitted sweater that Darla wore. The outfit came with a matching stretchy headband with a daisy affixed on top. The colors looked amazing with her brown skin and black hair.

"You're welcome," Lily said. "Dr. Edwards won't be long."

Sawyer worked to redress her quickly, and Darla went right back to sleep once she was snug in her three-piece outfit.

"Have you ever seen a baby more beautiful than ours?" Royce asked.

"No, but I bet every parent feels the same way."

Royce slipped his arm around Sawyer's lower back and said, "True, but we're right."

The exam room door swung open. Dr. Edwards entered the room and smiled down at the sleeping baby. "Good morning, dads. How's Miss Darla Grace doing?"

"Great," Sawyer said. "She's taking her bottles like a champ now."

"How many ounces is she drinking?" Dr. Edwards asked as she began her examination.

"Two and a half most feedings, but she's steadily climbing toward three," Sawyer replied.

"Plenty of wet diapers?"

"Oh yeah," Royce said. "Poops too."

Dr. Edwards smiled down at Darla, who'd just opened her eyes to see who was moving her legs and hips around. "That's what we want to hear." She carefully placed Darla on her stomach and turned her head until her cheek rested against the exam table. Their darling lifted her head just a little and mean-mugged the good doctor, who laughed. "This is what we want to see." She smiled at them. "Not the mad expressions so much as Darla building neck strength. Tummy time is crucial right from the jump. A lot of newborns don't like it unless they're lying on a parent's chest, which is fine with me. At least thirty minutes a day, but it doesn't have to be consecutive right now. And never leave them on their tummy unsupervised."

"Of course not," Sawyer agreed.

Dr. Edwards continued her examination, which included partially undressing the diva to check how her umbilical cord was doing. "Once this falls off, you can submerge her lower half in an infant tub and give her a true bath. Twice a week." She recommended different brands they could try and listed the ingredients they needed to stay away from if they wanted to try all-natural options. Sawyer planned to stick with the soaps, shampoos, powders, and lotions that parents had been using for decades. "How's Darla sleeping at night?"

"She isn't," Royce said.

"Ah," Dr. Edwards replied. "That's very common, even if frustrating, but you can shift her sleeping habits with a little effort and a lot of patience."

"Sawyer has a game plan, but we wanted to discuss it with you first," Royce said.

"Let's hear it," Dr. Edwards said.

"I think we're swaddling her too much during the day," Sawyer said. "We unwrap her to eat, of course, but I get hyperfixated on the room temperature and bundle her back up after she finishes her tummy time. I also read that it's best to keep the house bright during the day and to maintain normal daytime noise levels, but to keep the house darker and quiet at nighttime, especially during feedings."

"That's a solid plan," Dr. Edwards said. "Rely on low, soft lighting for overnight feedings, and don't turn on the television. Always have her sleep independently. Never with you in bed. She needs to be upright for twenty to thirty minutes after each bottle to digest, but at this stage, I would swaddle her and place her in a crib or bassinet afterward. Developing good sleep hygiene habits will set you up for a happy future. Some babies get too used to sleeping in someone's arms and don't want to sleep when you put them down. It's okay if she kicks up a little fuss or doesn't go to sleep right away. This gives her an opportunity to self-soothe and drift off to sleep. When she starts to wriggle and rock, you'll want to switch to a sleep sack instead of swaddling her. But we have some time before she's in jeopardy of rolling over."

"Darla is a Locke," Sawyer said. "So, I expect shenanigans at every stage."

"What about her weight loss?" Royce asked.

"It will probably take her a few weeks to get back to her birth weight, but that's typical for most newborns. Considering her initial issues with latching on, Darla is holding her own." She smiled at them. "You're off to a great start, guys. Do you have any questions for me?"

Sawyer and Royce exchanged a glance before shaking their heads.

"Great. We'll see you back for her one-month checkup," Dr. Edwards said.

"Thank you," they replied.

Once she left, they bundled Darla back into her carrier and lugged the massive diaper bag to the checkout area, where they scheduled Darla's routine visits for the next six months.

"Hungry?" Royce asked once they were back in the SUV.

"Starved," Sawyer replied. "Can we go through a drive-thru for greasy breakfast sandwiches and hash browns?"

"Hangover food?" Royce asked.

"More like sleep deprivation food." Sawyer looked over at Darla, who blinked against the daylight. "But you're worth it, baby girl. I've never been so happy to be this exhausted."

A vivid nightmare yanked Sawyer from his nap, and he jackknifed into a sitting position on the sofa. A cold sweat covered his face, and his heart galloped fast enough to steal his breath. He swallowed hard and blinked to bring his vision into focus. Tears filled his eyes when he saw Darla sleeping peacefully in the mobile bassinet beside him. Pressing a hand over his thundering heart, Sawyer willed himself to calm down and breathe.

Darla is here. She's safe. No one is going to take her away from us.

He kept repeating the same phrases until his pulse calmed and his breathing leveled out. Sawyer looked toward the recliner and was relieved that his near panic attack hadn't woken Royce from his nap either. The television played softly in the background, showing a television show he didn't recognize. The volume didn't seem to disturb Royce, so he carefully wheeled the bassinet into the kitchen so he could monitor Darla while he drank water and grabbed a snack.

A massive bowl of fruit sat on the counter, and that's where his attention should've gone, but he couldn't tear his gaze away from the bakery box next to it. Eating his emotions wouldn't solve a damn thing, but a jelly donut would sure as hell go down really well. Sawyer skipped the water, too, and poured himself a tall glass of milk. He leaned against the counter and intended to enjoy every bite and sip of his treat. Balance, he reminded himself. That was the key to a healthy life. He'd fix a nice big salad with grilled chicken and a lovely vinaigrette...and maybe some bacon and blue cheese crumbles on top. Yep, balance.

It was better to focus on the things he could control than the uncertainties that caused him to dream of people taking Darla away from them. The memory made tears well up, and Sawyer choked back a sob.

"No, damn it," he hissed. "I'm not doing this." He bit savagely into the donut, and blueberry jelly squished out of the back and plopped onto his shirt. "Just great."

Sawyer set his half-eaten pastry on top of the bakery box and attacked the jelly mess with a wet paper towel but only made it worse. The stain went from a small jelly blob to a large violet smear on the light gray fabric. He reached for the bassinet to wheel it into the laundry room with him but caught sight of the abandoned donut. "Well, we can't have that."

Sawyer wolfed it down in two more bites and knocked back his milk. His phone vibrated in his pocket, and he forgot all about the stain when he saw the name on the caller ID. Charlie Price. Sawyer's body went into that weird fear-response thing where he went hot and cold at the same time. Parts of him were burning with fever while others were frigid.

Breathe in. Breathe out. You're okay. Darla is safe. No one is taking her from you.

With his heart hammering in his throat, he answered the call before it rolled over to voicemail. "Hi, Charlie," he whispered.

"Is this a bad time?" Charlie whispered back.

Sawyer chuckled. "No. Darla and Royce are napping, but you don't have to whisper too."

"You should nap with them," Charlie said.

"I was, but I woke up and needed a snack. What's up?"

"I'm currently questioning my good judgment and probably my sanity too," Charlie replied.

That made Sawyer chuckle. "Still?"

"More so now than ever, but I made you a promise. You are a dear friend, and I love you like a brother, so despite my reservations, I have some updates for you." Charlie cleared his throat. "And this goes without saying, but I need this to stay between us."

"I won't breathe a word of this to anyone other than Royce," Sawyer promised.

"The person at the heart of the investigation is Shania Price. She's the owner of the adoption agency with the unethical practice allegations. I interviewed her within hours of the accident. Shania admitted to having a heated exchange with Ned Owens but denied threatening him with physical violence."

"No one ever admits to doing that," Sawyer said.

"To be fair, we only heard about those alleged threats through secondhand information."

"The bread and butter of most investigations," Sawyer pointed out.

"True, but I still have to prove it. The only irrefutable evidence right now is Shania's alibi. The woman has cameras on all the doors of her house, plus coverage of the driveway going all the way to the street. Their vehicles never moved, and both she and her husband were seen taking their dogs in and out to do their business at various times. The kids left for school and got on the bus at the end of the driveway. Shania and Peyton stayed home."

"Doesn't mean she's not responsible," Sawyer argued. "She could've hired it done or someone could've acted on her behalf out of misplaced loyalty."

"Yes, and that's why I'm trying to learn everything I can about Shania and Peyton. On the surface, everything looks good. They live within their means, they pay their bills on time, they have consistent work histories, and neither has a criminal record. There's nothing that jumps out or would justify a warrant to dig deeper. And I've had to be cautious about interviewing people they know because I don't want to tip them off. But I finally got lucky."

"How?"

Charlie chuckled and said, "The receptionist at the agency seemed very uncomfortable during our first interview at the office, so I managed to bump into her at the grocery store. Reese was nervous at first, but we bonded over our favorite chips in the snack aisle. That's when she suggested I look at Landen Jordan for Ned's death."

"Who's that?" Sawyer asked.

"Shania's stepbrother. He recently moved here from Atlanta, and Reese claims the two are very close. She even leaned in and whispered the last part, her wide-eyed expression telling me the salacious parts she didn't want to say out loud."

"Interesting," Sawyer said.

"Uh-huh. So, I prompted her for a little more. At first, she focused on how sleazy Landen is before launching into how much time the stepsiblings spent together and how uncomfortable their body language makes her feel."

"So, she thinks they're fu—" The word died on Sawyer's lips when he looked down at his innocent daughter. "Um, intimate."

Charlie chuckled, then said, "Cleaning up my language was one of the hardest things about becoming a dad. You learn some bad habits around the cop shop."

"Very true," Sawyer said, casting his gaze at the box of donuts on the counter.

"Anyway," Charlie said. "There's nothing illegal about having an affair, not even with your stepbrother, but I looked closer at this Landen Jordan character anyway. Reese thought he was bad news, and her intuition was spot on. The dude has an arrest record longer than my leg, and he's served time for boosting cars, receiving and selling stolen property, and assault. Turns out vice already had Landen on their radar because he works for a guy we suspect of running a chop shop from his auto repair garage. And guess whose previous employer in Atlanta is in prison for the same crime?"

"Landen."

"Yep," Charlie said. "Vice has documented Landen driving a dark late-model BMW with blacked-out windows. He usually comes and goes at night, so they're not sure if the car is black or navy blue. The woman who'd discovered Ned Owens on the side of the road is certain she encountered the vehicle that had struck him. She'd nearly collided with a dark blue or black sedan when it ran a stop sign and barreled through an intersection at high speeds. The windows had a dark tint, so she couldn't glimpse the driver, but she said there was clear damage to the front of the vehicle. She realized it had struck something and fled the scene. Her intuition told her that someone needed help, so she turned down that road instead of continuing forward. That's when she found Ned."

Sawyer rubbed a hand over his face instead of muttering the expletive that came so naturally to his tongue. "How terrible for her."

"Yeah, she was devastated," Charlie said. "I confirmed with Reese that she's seen Landen driving a navy blue BMW with blacked-out windows, so I'm positive we know who killed Ned Owens and why."

Hope flared in Sawyer's heart. "That's good news, Charlie."

"Don't congratulate me yet," his friend said. "Our suspects pulled a disappearing act before I could bring them into the station for an official interview."

Sawyer's heart fell. "Fuck." He wasn't about to apologize for that one. "Are all of them gone?"

"Yep. Peyton Price is an amateur racer who owns an RV and a car hauler he pulls behind it. According to the neighbors, it's usual for them to load up the kids and dogs and disappear for an extended period to attend an event somewhere in the US. But this time they took off in the middle of the night. When my detectives checked out the property, they looked in the garage and noted that the race car was inside it. Maybe they had more than one, or perhaps they took it out of the hauler so they could dispose of Landen's BMW somewhere it wouldn't get traced back to them."

"What kind of racing does he do?" Sawyer asked.

"Drag. He's plastered his social media accounts with photos from racetracks. Looks like he wins a lot."

"I watched a documentary about drag racing once, and that's one expensive hobby," Sawyer said. "That's probably the income-to-asset imbalance you're looking for. It wouldn't be glaringly obvious at first that they're spending more than their documented earnings." The possibility they'd profited from coercing disadvantaged women into giving up their babies was sickening. Had they turned to murder to prevent their exploitation from getting exposed? "What about the woman who'd come forward to Ned? Is she safe?"

"Yes, and more determined than ever to tell her truth. These people completely underestimated her if they thought killing Ned would intimidate her."

"Now what?" Sawyer asked.

"We've got enough to name them our primary suspects, so I've put out a nationwide BOLO since we don't know where they're headed. I plan to go public with information during a press conference this afternoon, hoping someone will spot them and turn them in. But I wanted to tell you first what we've discovered. I've also filed for a fuck ton of warrants to comb through every part of these people's lives and build a case for when they are captured."

"I appreciate you, Charlie."

"We're going to get them, buddy. This case is going to pick up national attention, and they're going to find it impossible to hide."

And Sawyer knew four prominent podcasters who could ensure the case received maximum exposure. But he had to wait until CCSD issued the information first to avoid stepping on Charlie's toes. He thanked his friend again, and they ended the call. Energy buzzed through Sawyer's body, making it impossible for him to lie down or even sit on the sofa. Charlie seemed to have a good handle on the investigation, and he already planned to lean on his friends to help spread the message. He needed to do more, but what?

Sawyer longed for a whiteboard and a dry-erase marker because writing things down always brought him clarity and inspired solutions. His gaze landed on the lawn sign his great-aunt had given them at their baby shower. It was white and had a cartoon stork carrying a baby in a blanket from its beak. The words below the bird made it very clear to any kidnappers that there was a newborn in residence. There was no way in hell they were going to stick that thing in front of their home.

He wheeled Darla into the dining area of the kitchen and turned the sign around to see if it had a graphic on the backside as well. Nope. It was a blank surface, and the corrugated plastic reminded him of a whiteboard. He darted back into the kitchen to see if he had a dry-erase marker or even a Sharpie to use. He came up empty there but found a pack of colorful sticky notes and a ballpoint pen.

"Even better," he whispered to Darla. "Daddy can throw away any of the sticky notes that don't make sense."

She wriggled in response, and he checked both the clock and the feeding schedule to see how close she was to her next bottle. They had an hour to go, which was plenty of time for him to noodle through his thoughts and unwrap Darla from her swaddling to encourage her to wake naturally. They'd learned the hard way that their beautiful butterfly didn't like to come out of her cocoon all at once. She wanted a slow, dramatic reveal.

Sawyer released the Velcro tabs from her torso and opened the little flaps but left the zipper alone. Darla wriggled her body and moved her head from side to side a few times, but she didn't scream in protest. She sighed and continued sleeping, so Sawyer eased back over to his makeshift whiteboard. He set a timer on his watch to unzip his princess and set to work. Fears, hunger, and frustration settled in the back of his mind, allowing the shrewd detective to take over. When the timer went off, he pivoted his attention back to Darla.

"It's time for stage two, Pumpkin." Sawyer held his breath as he eased the zipper down the front of the swaddling sleep sack. "No need to be angry with Daddy. It's time to wake up and be alert for your bottle." He unzipped her without pissing her off and did a silent happy dance. Darla wriggled, stretched her precious arms and legs, and arched her back. She made a rooting motion with her head, smacked her little lips, and then settled back into sleep. She had another twenty minutes before she was due to eat, so he left her to wake on her own and set a new timer. He had only a few more notes to make or suggestions to offer, though he wouldn't give those to Charlie unless asked. Probably.

"Whatcha doing?" Royce whispered behind him.

Sawyer hadn't heard him approach, so he gasped and triggered a regretful chain of events. Darla woke with a scream, Dolly barked from the living room, and Bones was likely plotting to murder them all. He spun around to face Royce, who'd picked Darla up to soothe her. Sawyer felt like a complete monster for upsetting her. Tears filled his eyes as he watched Royce rub her tiny back. Their gazes met and held. "I don't think I'm very good at this," Sawyer said.

Royce looked at the notes he'd made before shifting his gaze to

Sawyer. "At taking time off work? And you thought I'd be the restless one."

"No, I'm terrible at parenting," Sawyer said. "I traumatized her."

Snorting, Royce shook his head. "You did no such thing. All parents startle their babies and feel like assholes afterward." His eyes widened when he realized what he'd said. "You don't realize how often you cuss until you try to quit." Royce tipped his head to the makeshift whiteboard. "What case are you working on?"

"Ours."

Royce responded with a quirked brow, so Sawyer filled him in on the conversation he'd had with Charlie and his plans to involve their podcasting friends. His husband's mouth curved into a wry smile, and he lowered his head to Darla's ear and whispered, "Sitting back and letting others take the lead makes your daddy very uncomfortable, even when they're equally qualified for the tasks. Some people call him a control freak, but we'll call him relentless."

Sawyer's shoulders sagged as he sighed. "I just can't let this go. Doing something feels proactive, while waiting leads to…"

"Scary thoughts?"

Sawyer recalled the nightmare that had woken him from his nap. All the fear and anguish he'd felt resurfaced, balling up to form a lump in his throat. He nodded when the words wouldn't come and exhaled the negative emotions on his next breath. "I dreamed someone came to take Darla away from us," Sawyer admitted. "It was so vivid and terrifying."

Royce's gaze turned sympathetic, and he tugged Sawyer forward with his free hand. "Time for a family hug." He slung his arm around Sawyer's waist and held him close. Darla had nodded off against Royce's chest, and Sawyer laid his head against the opposite shoulder to gaze at their daughter and soak in the love they shared.

"No one is going to take our daughter away from us," Royce said. "This I can promise. Our situation isn't like the other ones Ivy described to us. We sought legal counsel prior to conceiving Darla. Kelsey had her own legal representation to ensure her rights were respected. We have dozens of character witnesses to go to bat for us and countless receipts to show that Kelsey entered the arrangement of her own free will. Most importantly, Kelsey supports us completely. What happened to the young lady at the heart of the allegations is terrible, and my heart goes out to her, but our situation isn't the same. Our adoption might get delayed, but I promise you it will happen. We will end up with a lawful adoption decree and a birth certificate naming us both as Darla Grace Locke's parents. No one is destroying our family, and I won't entertain any other thoughts."

Sawyer clung to Royce's fierce conviction as tightly as he hugged his powerful body. "As it was declared, so it shall be."

Royce pressed a kiss to his temple. "Period."

CHAPTER NINE

ROYCE LOOKED AT DARLA AND SHOOK HIS HEAD IN DISMAY. "Maybe we should've waited longer than a week before allowing visitors," he called out to Sawyer and Evangeline, who were busy trying to find refrigerator and freezer space for the food their friends and family had brought.

"Most of this stuff will freeze just fine," Evangeline said. "You'll appreciate the surplus once you've gone back to work and have to cook dinner after a long day."

"I don't doubt that, and I appreciate everyone's thoughtfulness," Royce said. "My issue isn't with the food gifts."

Sawyer walked to the edge of the kitchen and frowned. "What's wrong?"

Royce crooked a finger at him in response. "Come see for yourself."

"I want to see too," Evangeline said as she blew past Sawyer.

Mother and son joined Royce by the bassinet. One snickered, and the other sucked in an outraged breath.

"We were very clear that we didn't want people kissing Darla," Sawyer said, pointing at the bright red lip print on the center of their daughter's forehead. "Who did this?"

Evangeline bit her lip to keep from laughing. "I'm sorry. I know it's not funny, and yes, you made your feelings crystal clear." A small giggle escaped before she could stop it. "But it seems one of your great-aunts left a little F-you on their way out the door."

"That will be the last time Dad springs them from the home to visit Darla." Sawyer raised his hands in surrender. "I'm not trying to be an asshole, control freak, or a germaphobe, but this is unacceptable behavior. Darla is ten days old, and she doesn't need people breathing their germs on her."

Royce wished he'd just wiped the lipstick off her forehead without showing Sawyer. He was also irritated that people hadn't respected their wishes, but he feared Sawyer's underlying anxiety would make this a bigger issue than it needed to be. Royce took out a wet wipe, hoping a quick swipe would remove the makeup and cut Sawyer off at the pass, but he only smeared the red lips on Darla's forehead.

Evangeline slapped a hand over her mouth and turned her back to them, but her shoulders shook with suppressed laughter.

"Mom!" Sawyer hissed. "It's not funny. We don't know a thing about removing makeup. How do we get this off?" Then Sawyer turned to Royce. "Do you see the humor in this?"

His wild-eyed outrage triggered a fit of laughter that started deep in Royce's belly. It rumbled and tumbled, building speed until it burst from his mouth in huge guffaws. Royce pressed a hand to his stomach as he tried to get himself under control. Evangeline blew out a few breaths, giggled some more, and then finally turned around. She and Royce locked eyes, and they gave in to another fit of laughter.

"It's not funny," Royce said between gasps. "He's absolutely right about the germs, and we don't want those makeup chemicals on our daughter's skin."

Evangeline rested her hand on Royce's shoulder and inhaled shakily. "I know. Sawyer is absolutely right." But then she pointed to the lipstick smear on Darla's forehead, and they set off again.

"A giant F-you," Royce.

"That looks like my Aunt Edith's signature red shade," Evangeline said.

Sawyer gasped. "I bet you're right. She's the same one who gave us the yard sign to advertise we had a baby to any potential kidnappers." He pointed at Darla's head and added, "Aunt Edith did that to get even because we didn't put her sign in our lawn."

They'd just settled down when Sawyer looked between them in utter disbelief and did the absolute worst thing possible. He stomped his foot and set them off again.

"His foot," Evangeline husked out, fully leaning on Royce for support by this time.

"I've never seen that reaction before," Royce replied.

Evangeline righted herself and sucked in huge gulps of air. "I haven't seen it since he was an angry toddler."

That remark tickled Royce's funny bone again, but he kept himself together. He hadn't spent a lot of time wondering how little Sawyer behaved when he was angry. Royce just figured he smoldered like the adult version, but maybe not as intensely. "He stomped his foot?"

"Like a bull before it charges," Evangeline said.

Sawyer rolled his eyes as he cut in front of Royce and wheeled the bassinet away.

"Where are you going?" Evangeline asked.

"While you two were yucking it up, I searched the internet for the solution to our lipstick dilemma," Sawyer replied.

"I hate to see him go, but I love to watch him leave," Royce said, adding a whistle that made Evangeline giggle. "You did good work with that one."

"I know," Evangeline said.

"I just can't with you two," Sawyer said before he disappeared down the hallway with Darla.

Evangeline patted Royce's shoulder. "I'd better go with him. I want to make sure he's taking our teasing in the spirit it's intended. Sawyer seems a little edgier than usual."

Royce sighed. "Yeah. He's trying to stay positive, but knowing our adoption will probably get delayed is taking its toll. And it doesn't help that the suspects in the case have eluded the authorities for over a week. The guys from the *Sinister in Savannah* podcast and Alec have made a major push to get the info out to their wide-reaching audiences, but still nothing. Their inevitable arrests won't change our outcome, but we can't stand the injustice of it all. The accusations about the adoption agency and the law firm representing them have gone public, and the damage is done. It's now a matter of waiting to see if a judge reviews all the adoptions handled by the law firm during a certain time or only the ones involving the adoption agency."

"It's an awful mess," Evangeline said. "I imagine it's hard for two cynical police officers to have blind faith that things will work out, but I believe enough for all of us."

"Thanks, Mama," Royce said, kissing her cheek.

He sat down on the couch and turned the television on for the first time since their guests had arrived after breakfast. The visitors hadn't all come at once, just a steady stream of well-wishers and at least one rogue baby kisser. To have so many people supporting them was a blessing, but Royce was excited to take his house back. And then the doorbell rang.

Dolly leaped up from her spot beside him on the couch, barking her head off. Royce braced himself for Darla to wake up, but no cries came from the hallway. He scooped Dolly up, kissed her on top of the head, and took her with him to answer the door.

"All right, killer. Let's go see who's here." Her little body vibrated with a growl, but she didn't bark again. Royce opened the door and greeted the couple standing on the porch. It took him a minute to recognize the men sporting golden tans and relaxed smiles. "Chief," he said. "I thought you were out of town on vacation with Mr. Chief."

Abe snorted and looked at Mendoza. "Guess that makes us Mr. and Mr. Sheriff too."

Mendoza rolled his eyes heavenward and extended an enormous paper carryout bag. "We got back last night, which is why I didn't have time to prepare something for you from scratch."

"Dodged one there, buddy," Abe said with a wink.

Mendoza cut him a dark look, but his eyes shimmered with humor. "You don't look like you're starving to me."

Abe patted his stomach. "Not after the vacation we've just had."

Royce watched their byplay in awe. Mendoza was the most private person he'd ever met, so getting a glimpse beyond the wall fascinated him. But his entertainment ended as quickly as it began. Mendoza seemed to recall where he was, and the shield went up again.

"We just wanted to stop by with some food and congratulate you in person," Mendoza said. "Those first few weeks with a newborn are rough, and I figured you guys could use a meal you didn't have to cook."

"Thank you," Royce said as he accepted the bag. "We appreciate it very much. Would you like to come in and meet the baby?"

"This isn't her?" Abe teased, nodding toward Dolly.

"No, but she thinks so." Royce kissed the dog's head and made quick introductions before stepping aside so they could enter. "Sawyer and his mother are trying to get lipstick off Darla's forehead," he said as he led them into the living room. "You might see a side of my husband you didn't know existed." Though Sawyer would be on his best behavior in front of Chief Mendoza and Abe. "We communicated a 'no kissing' rule to our guests this morning, and one of his elderly aunts left a bright red lip print on her forehead. He's livid."

"Can't blame him," Mendoza said. "No one wants people breathing nasty germs and bacteria onto their babies. It's flu season, for crying out loud."

"Make yourselves comfortable," Royce said, gesturing to the couch. "I'll just go put the food in the kitchen."

He set Dolly down on the floor, and she immediately jumped onto Abe's lap, turning the brawny sheriff into putty. Traitorous trollop. He unpacked the bag and looked at the contents in each aluminum pan to decide if it was something they'd want to freeze for later or eat soon. Abe and Mendoza had basically delivered a holiday feast to their house. Royce shifted the lasagna to the freezer to make room for the spiral-cut ham and all its glorious trimmings. He nearly dropped the mashed potatoes on the floor when he heard Mendoza fawning over Dolly. He peeked around the door and caught his chief making kissy faces at the dog and wished he hadn't left his phone on the coffee table. Sawyer still hadn't returned to the living room, and there was no way in hell he'd believe Royce's claims without evidence. Knowing Mendoza wouldn't want Royce to witness this too-human moment, he finished shuffling food and shut the refrigerator door harder than necessary to warn his chief that he was coming back. But he put a little too much oomph into it because a chunk of ice fell out of the dispenser and onto the floor. And it turned out the gesture was uncalled for since Mendoza was standing just on the other side of the door when he'd closed it. Royce yelped in surprise. "Didn't hear you sneak up on me, Chief."

"He's light on his feet like a panther," Abe called out from the living room. "And silent as smoke."

"Did you need something?" Royce asked.

The smile Mendoza gave him was pure predator. "Could I have something to drink?"

"Of course. Soda, juice, water, or something stronger?"

"Water would be great."

"Still or sparkling? Flavored or unflavored?"

Mendoza's brow furrowed. "Anything unflavored."

"Coming right up." Royce stepped back, and his foot landed on the slippery ice. His leg slid out from under him, and he slammed into the refrigerator hard enough to dislodge something from the top, which slid down the side. "Well, damn." Royce peered into the thin gap between the appliance and wall, but it was too dark to see. Reaching into the abyss, his fingers brushed against something thin and plastic. "What the hell?"

Royce didn't recognize what it was until he pulled the item from the gap, and his gaze landed on the colorful sticky notes plastered all over it. He turned it over before Mendoza recognized Sawyer's murder board and came face-to-face with a smiling stork.

"What the hell's that?" Mendoza asked, pointing at the sign.

"It's a cartoon stork, Chief. It's a common symbol people use to welcome newborns into a family."

"Yeah, I know what a stork represents," Mendoza replied. "I'm talking about the sticky notes on the back. Pretty sure I saw headings that read 'suspects' and 'evidence' above them." Of course, eagle-eyed Mendoza spotted Sawyer's makeshift murder board. "Are you guys running active investigations while on paternity leave? Tell me you're not doing that."

"We are not doing that," Royce said.

Mendoza narrowed his eyes and gestured for Royce to give him the sign. He could've refused to hand it over since they were standing in his kitchen, but Mendoza's steely-eyed expression conveyed that absolute compliance was the only option.

"It's not what you think, Chief."

Abe entered the kitchen with Dolly tucked under his arm. "It never is."

Mendoza's dark gaze raked over Sawyer's notes before snapping up to meet Royce's eyes. "This is exactly what I thought it was." He turned it so Abe could see. "And I think this proprietary and confidential information belongs to your department."

One of Abe's golden brows shot up, but curiosity reflected in his expression instead of anger. He was the arctic chill to Mendoza's raging inferno. "So it is. And it doesn't take a genius to know where you've gotten this information." Abe's calm acceptance only seemed to fuel Mendoza's outrage.

"Why aren't you angry? Your undersheriff shared confidential information about an ongoing investigation with his former partner."

Abe shrugged. "Why are you angry? I seem to recall a time when you asked me to bend the rules to rescue this one"—Abe hooked a thumb in Royce's direction—to clarify who he'd meant.

That took a little starch out of the chief's expression. "I was only a deputy chief back then."

"Lio," Abe said, drawing out his nickname while shaking his head. "Ease up."

Mendoza narrowed his eyes and studied his husband. "You already knew that Charlie had shared the information with Sawyer."

"Yes, I'd had several messages from Charlie when I turned my phone back on after landing at the airport. I'd have done the same thing in his shoes, and you would have too." Abe looked at Royce and said, "I strongly recommend turning off your phones during vacations. It's life-changing."

"Noted," Royce said.

"Did I hear my name?" Sawyer called from the living room before Royce could send a signal for his husband to save himself. He'd been more than willing to fall on the sword for whatever punishment their chief wanted to eke out, but Mendoza knew exactly where the information had come from and the likely recipient. They'd both have their heads on the chopping block for this.

"Run," Royce joked. "Save yourself."

Sawyer scowled for a few seconds until he saw what Mendoza held in his hand. Either he hoped the baby would soften their chief's reaction or he'd forgotten he still gripped the bassinet, because he wheeled Darla into the kitchen with him. "I can explain." Unfortunately for him, Evangeline was only a step behind her son.

She read only a few of the notes before putting it all together. "Sawyer," she hissed, rounding on him. "Tell me you're not involving yourself in Charlie's investigation."

Mendoza handed Royce the makeshift murder board and eased back a few steps. It was the first time Royce had ever seen him look nervous. "We should probably get going."

"But we just got here," Abe complained. He leaned over the bassinet and smiled down at Darla. "And I want to hold the baby."

"Royce," Evangeline said, "you take your guests into the living room so they can hold Darla while I have a chat with my son."

"Yes, ma'am." He'd been prepared to take the full brunt of Mendoza's anger, but he'd happily escape Evangeline's wrath. He eased the bassinet from Sawyer's grip, kissed his husband's cheek, and gestured for Mendoza and Abe to follow him to the living room. "Oh," he said, stopping suddenly, "I forgot to grab your water from the refrigerator, Chief."

"I'm fine," Mendoza said. It seemed not even their badass chief was immune to maternal outrage. He cut a glance in Sawyer's direction and said, "Guess he's getting punished enough for meddling in a case outside our jurisdiction. I can let this slide."

Abe bit his bottom lip to keep from laughing, then led their little parade into the living room. He made himself comfortable on the couch and passed Dolly over to Mendoza, who held the dog at eye level and told her she wasn't allowed to lick him. Dolly let out an outraged yip and did it anyway, catching him on the cheek before he could dodge her.

"Your dog is a lot like you, Locke," Mendoza declared.

"I haven't licked anyone who didn't want it," Royce replied.

Mendoza's face turned pink, and he muttered, "You know what I meant."

"You set yourself up for that," Abe said as he smiled down at Darla in the bassinet. He pumped hand sanitizer into his palm from the industrial-sized bottle Sawyer kept on the coffee table and vigorously rubbed his hands together. Abe eased the baby from her bassinet and said, "Isn't that right, sweet angel? Uncle Lio stepped right into that one."

Uncle Lio? Royce figured stranger things could happen than his chief becoming so familiar with Darla that she'd call him an uncle, but there weren't many. Mendoza didn't reject the notion outright, but he was too spellbound by his husband holding the tiny infant. The chief's guard was down, and his expression was pure love.

"Don't hog her to yourself," Mendoza said.

"I've only held her for like two minutes. Kiss the dog and wait your turn."

In the most shocking turn of the day, Mendoza kissed Dolly on the top of her head. He must've sensed Royce gawking at him because he curled his lips in a snarl. "Problem?"

"No, sir. Just don't leave lipstick on her fur."

"I'll do my best," Mendoza replied dryly.

Royce looked into the kitchen to see how Sawyer was faring with Evangeline, but the dustup was already over. She passed the makeshift murder board back to Sawyer, kissed his cheek, and grabbed her purse off the kitchen island. She blew Royce a kiss and then headed down the hallway toward the garage with Sawyer following behind her, wearing a hangdog expression on his handsome face.

"Oh, hey!" Abe said. "That's Trixie Mattel. What are you watching?"

Royce turned back to the television and saw a very tall drag queen with big boobs, enormous blonde hair, and exaggerated makeup that made her look like a doll. "Um, I don't know. We were checking out a hilarious show called *English Teacher* before our friends and family arrived. I might've resumed the show by accident." The scene changed to include a group of high school boys gaping at the drag queen. Royce hit Pause on the remote, and the show's name and episode title came up on the screen. He had started the next episode of *English Teacher*, but he hadn't gotten far. "Oops. I better go back to the beginning and wait for Sawyer."

"Good show?" Mendoza asked.

"Great so far," Royce replied.

Mendoza nodded. "Is Trixie in every episode? She's my favorite."

"Your favorite actor?" Royce asked.

"Drag queen."

Royce couldn't imagine Mendoza watching drag queen

performances, let alone having a favorite. "Interesting." The chief's scowl made him realize he'd spoken that out loud.

"You don't watch *Drag Race?*" Mendoza asked.

Royce shook his head. "Just the kind that involves cars."

"That's not nearly as entertaining," Mendoza told him. "You've got three months off work, so it would be a perfect time to watch the franchise."

"Franchise?" Royce asked.

"It started with a single series in the US before moving to the UK, Canada, and far beyond," Abe said.

"Both of you love it?" Royce asked.

"More than sports," Abe replied. "Hearing these queens talk about the bigotry they've faced and how hard they've struggled to find acceptance really gets to you."

Mendoza nodded before adding, "But then you get stories of unconditional love, and you realize that humanity still exists."

"Sounds like those tear-jerking backstories they tell before every Super Bowl," Royce said.

"It's exactly like that," Abe replied. "Except you get at least one or two backstories every episode while they're getting ready for their main stage presentations. I think that's my favorite part of the show."

"Same," Mendoza agreed. "One minute, you're grumbling about a shady-ass queen, and the next, you're cheering for them to win the crown and the cash."

Royce looked from one husband to the other. Was he dreaming this conversation?

"Now, give me that baby, and no one will get hurt," Mendoza said. He set Dolly on the couch, sanitized his hands, and held out his arms for Darla. The exchange was peaceful, and no one lost a limb.

"You sound like my mom when someone holds Darla too long," Sawyer said as he rejoined them. "About that murder board..."

Mendoza waved him away with his free hand. "No explanations needed. I trust you."

Royce expected to hear harpsichord music and see a beam of angelic benevolence shine upon his husband's head.

"Thank you," Sawyer said, then turned to Abe. "I promise I'm not interfering in your investigation. I jot down thoughts to keep my brain from turning them over on an endless loop."

"I understand. Charlie told me he's kept you updated, and I don't have a problem with it. I'd want the same thing if our situations were reversed."

"Thank you." Sawyer noticed the paused television screen and asked if they'd watched *English Teacher*.

Abe and Mendoza told him they hadn't yet, then launched into another impassioned endorsement of *RuPaul's Drag Race*.

"Alec loves that show," Sawyer said. "He swears I'll love it too, but I'm more of a documentary man."

"Give it a shot," Abe said. "And don't judge the entire franchise on the weird camera filter they use in season one."

They chatted for a while longer until Darla woke up from her nap, looking for her next bottle. She nuzzled against Mendoza's chest, and he laughed.

"Can't help you, kid," he said, offering her back to Royce.

"I'll warm up her bottle," Sawyer said.

"We should get going." Abe stood and hauled Mendoza by his hand.

"We need to tackle laundry and groceries and all the boring things I did not miss during vacation," Mendoza said. "Enjoy these precious months at home with Darla. They'll go by so fast." He cocked his head to the side. "Before you know it—"

"Nope," Royce said, cutting him off. He didn't want to think about how quickly time would pass. "I just have this moment right here, and I'll never get it back."

Abe clapped him on the back. "There you go." He gestured to the kitchen, where Sawyer was readying Darla's bottle. "Don't let him lose sight of that. I want you guys to enjoy being first-time fathers and let my department worry about the Ned Owens investigation."

"Yes, sir."

Royce, Darla, and Dolly saw them to the door before returning to the couch, where Sawyer waited for them with a warm bottle. He had a Boppy pillow on his lap and a soft spit-up towel draped over one shoulder. Sawyer's brown eyes were warm, free of fear, and full of hope. "You've never looked more beautiful to me than you do right now."

"You're being silly," Sawyer said.

"No, I'm not. Fatherhood looks so damn good on you."

"Not as good as it looks on you," Sawyer said.

And they grinned at each other like fools until Darla kicked up a fuss. Royce handed her to Sawyer and smiled as he positioned her the way she liked. They were so perfect together. It would be so easy to imagine what their life could look like in one year, five years, or even ten. But he wouldn't allow it. Royce had this one breathtaking moment, and it was all he needed.

CHAPTER TEN

SAWYER PRESSED RECORD AND DISCREETLY AIMED HIS CELL phone in Royce's direction as RuPaul prepared to name the season two winning queen. Royce had his heart set on Raven taking the crown, but Sawyer had stumbled across enough Reddit rants to know that would not happen. Sawyer kept his head aimed toward the television but shifted his gaze to the recliner, where Royce lounged with their sleeping daughter.

"Come on," Royce mumbled. "Crown Raven already." He chewed his bottom lip as RuPaul built tension on the screen. There was a dramatic pause, and then Ru announced Tyra as the winner. "*What?*" Royce stage-whispered. Darla's little arms went up in the air like she was signaling a touchdown, but she didn't wake up. Dolly didn't bark. Bones didn't flee from Sawyer's lap. Royce patted Darla's back and kissed the top of her head. "Papa's sorry, baby girl." Royce scowled in his direction, and Sawyer expected to be called out for recording his reaction. But he said, "Why aren't you outraged?"

"Raven is stunning and my first pick, but the judges were enamored by Tyra," Sawyer said casually.

"No, there's more to it than that." Royce studied him through narrowed eyes, and Sawyer barely resisted the urge to laugh. "You already knew the outcome."

"Guilty. I didn't mean to find the results, but I came across them when researching something else about the franchise." Sawyer tapped the phone to stop the recording and quickly texted it to Alec with a message that read, *Look what you've done!* Technically, Sawyer could lay their newest obsession at Mendoza's feet, but Alec was the first person in their inner circle to push the show.

"Did you record my reaction?" Royce asked.

"Yep."

Royce's mouth fell open in outrage. "Did you just send that to someone?"

"Alec," Sawyer replied. "He'll be happy to know we're addicted to the show too." Sawyer's phone buzzed with an incoming call, and Alec's name on the screen wasn't a surprise.

"You've got five minutes to chat before I'm starting season three," Royce said.

Sawyer bit his lip to keep from laughing. "You don't want to stretch or hydrate?"

Royce rubbed Darla's back. "I'm good just like this."

Sawyer accepted the call and greeted Alec. He stood up to get a drink and noticed how messy their house had become since Darla's arrival three weeks prior. They weren't living in squalor as they adjusted to life with a newborn, but the clutter was making Sawyer's skin itch. Maybe he should do something about it instead of watching reality television when they weren't sleeping or at least attempt a healthier balance. "Where are you right now?"

"Amarillo," Alec replied.

Sawyer sang lyrics about arriving in Amarillo by morning.

"I didn't know you could sing," Alec said.

"And I didn't realize I knew that song. Couldn't even tell you who sings it."

"George Strait," Alec replied. "A legend."

"I'll take your word for it," Sawyer told him. "How's it going?"

"Rough. These Texas boys are suspicious as hell and don't want to play nice. Not everyone rolls out a red carpet like you guys did."

"Wow, that's some revisionist history right there," Sawyer teased.

Alec laughed, and Sawyer imagined him rolling his eyes. "Okay, sure. We had a rough start, but I wore you down."

"Because you eventually allowed us to see the real Alec Bishop," Sawyer said. "Maybe you should do the same there. Perhaps strike up a conversation about *Drag Race* at the water cooler."

Alec gay gasped through their connection. "Can you imagine?"

"Actually, yes, and I take it back."

"Because you like me and don't want to see me hurt," Alec said. "It's okay to admit it."

Sawyer and Royce had both formed a surprisingly tight bond with Alec. "Fine. I admit it."

"So, you're obsessed with *Drag Race*, aren't you?"

"Obsessed is a stretch." But then Sawyer noted the clutter on his kitchen counters. "Maybe a little," he amended.

"Darla seemed very indifferent to the results," Alec said. "A real snooze fest to her. *Ba-dum-tss*. I'll be here all week, ladies and gentlemen."

Sawyer laughed at Alec's shenanigans, then said, "She only cared about cuddling her papa."

"So," Alec said, "have you seen Dane and Cayden recently?"

"I have. They brought pizza by last week and met Darla Grace." Sunday dinner was a tradition they'd started with Dane, Cayden, and their mom, Nina, and they'd continued hosting the brothers after her passing. That, along with cleaning, was a healthy routine Sawyer was eager to start up again. A quick glance at his phone told him it was Friday afternoon, which gave them plenty of time to tidy the house and thaw out one of the many casseroles from the freezer.

"You got quiet suddenly," Alec said. "Where'd you go?"

"Sorry. My focus is crap right now."

"I bet. Is Darla still staying awake all night?" Alec asked.

"No, she's doing better. Royce and I should take turns with the late-night feedings, but we're too obsessed with her. One of us changes her diaper while the other prepares the bottle. We both stare at her like fools, marveling over every little thing. We're kind of ridiculous."

"I think it's adorable how much you love her," Alec said. Their conversation lulled for a few seconds, and Sawyer wondered if their connection had broken, but Alec cleared his throat. "How are Dane and Cayden doing?"

"They're hanging in there as best as brokenhearted young men can," Sawyer said. "Of course, they miss their mom like crazy, but they're putting one foot in front of the other as she'd instructed them. They've both made room in their grief for new and exciting things."

"Like love?" Alec asked.

Sawyer wondered how to proceed. Alec and Dane had an undeniable attraction to one another, but the timing had been terrible. He didn't want to give Alec false hope, but he didn't want his friend to mope needlessly either. "Cay has his first girlfriend. They went to the winter formal together last month, and the budding relationship seems to have helped him quite a bit."

"What about Dane?" It seemed Alec was tired of skirting around the actual issue. "Is he seeing someone?"

"Why don't you ask Dane that? He said you guys talk and text all the time."

"We do," Alec said. "But he's been...different lately. A little distant."

"Could be a self-preservation tactic. Maybe Dane was becoming more emotionally involved with you than he could handle. We both know he cares about you a great deal."

Alec sighed heavily. "And I'm in love with him. My gut tells me to ease up and give him space to heal, but my heart wants me to hold on tighter."

"I think you need to let Dane set the tone and pace," Sawyer said. "I know that's the last thing you want to hear."

"No, but it's the reminder I needed. Dane wants me to be his friend, and I can be that for him. It's just hard being on the other side of the country."

"But that's a temporary problem," Sawyer pointed out. "There's nothing preventing you from moving to Savannah once your mission is over. Sometimes you just have to believe that things will work out the way they're intended. As much as we like to be in charge, we're not really steering the ship."

Alec chuckled. "Was that little pep talk for me or for yourself?"

"Both." Lord knew he needed the reminder every day that passed without a resolution on the case, or even a word from the judge about their adoption hearing. They'd gone through all the motions and completed all the outstanding tasks. Waiting was the only thing left to do.

Royce met Sawyer's gaze, pointed to the television, and held up two fingers. He needed to wrap up the call before Royce started the next season, or they wouldn't get anything accomplished for another few days. Muffled voices came from Alec's side of the connection, followed by his friend's heavy sigh.

"I need to go," Alec said. "The sheriff has finally granted me an audience, but he's only giving me five minutes to make my case."

"To quote Mama Ru," Sawyer said, "'Good luck, and don't fuck it up.'"

Alec was laughing when he disconnected their call, and Sawyer hoped that good energy would follow his friend into the meeting with the sheriff.

Royce waved the remote at him, and his expression said he meant serious business. Sawyer did too, but he'd need reinforcement to pull it off. And he knew just who to call.

Twenty minutes later, Royce crossed his arms over his chest and scowled at the diaper bag Sawyer had packed. "I don't know about this."

Sawyer cocked his head to the side. "You don't trust my mom to watch Darla for a few hours?" He knew it was a low blow, but desperate times called for devious measures.

Evangeline wore the diaper bag slung over one shoulder and a serene smile on her face. She glanced down at her granddaughter and said, "He doesn't trust me with you."

Royce's eyes widened in alarm. "You know that's not true at all. This is just her first time away from us, and I…" His words trailed off as he looked around the room, and Sawyer could tell by his horrified expression that he was seeing what had become of their living space. "I think we're going to use the time wisely."

"Perfect," Evangeline said. "Sawyer has packed enough diapers, outfits, and formula for her to stay for a month, but I promise to bring her back as soon as you call me." She smiled down at Darla, who stared up at her in awe. "That way, your daddies will call on me to watch you more often, though I suspect I'll have to share you with Grandpa Eddie when you get bigger. I hear he's already planning your first trip to the hardware store."

"I'll walk you out and double-check the car seat installation," Sawyer said. They'd bought extra bases for Darla's car seat to make it easy to switch vehicles. Royce had installed one in both of their vehicles and Evangeline's too. "I'll be right back," Sawyer said. "You can get started if you want."

"I'm okay with waiting," Royce said, but he scanned the room as if trying to find the best place to jump in.

"You boys are being too hard on yourselves," Evangeline said as she led the way to her car. "Your home looks like you've just had a baby."

"While I know that's true, I also know that we're going to be judged much harsher than a hetero couple going through the second-parent adoption process."

Evangeline sighed. "I wish I could dispute your claim, but I suspect it's true." She opened the back seat and clicked the carrier into the base. "I really hate that you feel such unnecessary pressure." Evangeline stepped aside so Sawyer could make sure Darla was secure.

He ducked inside the back seat to perform a quick inspection, then smiled down at his little girl. "Have fun with Grandma. I love you so much." He kissed her forehead and eased out of the car. "She's all set. Thank you for doing this."

Evangeline pulled him into a tight hug. "It's my pleasure." She eased back and smiled up at him, mirth shimmering in her eyes. "And speaking of pleasure..."

"No," Sawyer said as he backed away.

Evangeline fixed an innocent expression on her face as she shut the car door. "What? I'm just saying you shouldn't burn all your energy on household chores. Self-care is critical at times like this."

"Okay," Sawyer said, saluting her with two fingers. "I'm taking your advice into consideration."

"And sex is wonderful self-care," Evangeline suggested as she walked around to the driver's side.

Sawyer spun around and walked back to the house. The first thing he noticed when he stepped inside was the fit of Royce's gray sweatpants as he bent over to declutter the coffee table. He had an empty trash bag in one hand and some snack cake wrappers in the other. Damn, what a beautiful sight. Sawyer was worried that he might be just as turned on by Royce's cleaning as the snug fit of his sweatpants. And that just wouldn't do. He moved closer, standing directly behind Royce to get the best view of the muscular swells under the soft cotton. No underwear lines. Even better.

Sensing Sawyer's nearness, Royce looked over his shoulder and froze. "Oh! I know that look."

"Mm-hmm."

Royce straightened and spun around too fast, swaying for a few seconds before he righted himself. That delay was enough for Sawyer to swoop in and untie his sweatpants. "What are..." The words turned to moans when Sawyer went to his knees. Royce dropped the trash bag and snack detritus on the ground, and Sawyer was too horny to care. Royce slid a hand into Sawyer's hair, tightening his fingers at the roots. "Should we?"

"We definitely should." They'd stolen a few moments here and there while Darla slept, but their intimacy had become quick, mutual handjobs in the shower. Sawyer wanted to take his time and relearn every inch of Royce's body, starting with his favorite part. He hooked his thumbs into Royce's waistband and dragged his pants down to mid-thigh. Leaning forward, Sawyer placed a kiss on the tip of Royce's cock. "But feel free to say no."

Royce's stormy eyes shimmered with a heat Sawyer had been sorely missing. "As if."

Parting his lips, Sawyer leaned forward and licked his husband's dick like it was the most delicious Popsicle ever made. He took his time along the sensitive underside and swirled his tongue around the head, moaning as Royce became fully erect in his mouth. Sawyer pulled back and looked up at Royce. "I really needed this."

Royce's lips curved into a wry smile. "And here I thought you wanted to clean. Is that the new code word?"

Sawyer chuckled as he stood up. "I still want to clean, but I need you more." He tugged Royce's pants up so he wouldn't trip and then led him to their bedroom.

"Ohhh, what are you going to do to me?" Royce asked.

"Everything. Take off your clothes."

Royce slid his sweatpants down his legs and kicked them to the side before yanking his shirt off and tossing it. "Your turn. Hurry"

"There's no need to rush. Evangeline won't bring Darla home until we call her." Yet Sawyer stripped down with equal vigor, though it took him a little longer since he had more layers of clothes to remove. "I want to take our time and—" Royce tackled him before he could finish, and Sawyer landed on the mattress with an "*oof.*"

Royce nuzzled his mouth against Sawyer's pulse point with a sexy growl. "I really want to oof you too."

Arousal flared red-hot and wild between them. Hands explored, mouths kissed, and dicks leaked with excitement, kicking primal urges into a higher gear, and Sawyer realized that taking it slow was the worst idea he'd ever had. "Okay," he said, wrapping his legs around Royce's waist. "New strategy."

Royce kissed a path up his neck and nibbled his earlobe. "I'm listening."

"You take me now. Hard and fast. Show me no mercy."

Rolling his hips, Royce hummed his approval. "And then…"

"You fill my ass with your spunk."

"I like it." Royce gripped Sawyer's ass and spread his cheeks. A wicked finger slid along his ass crack and tapped against his pucker. "Here?"

"Yes, get the lube."

But Royce didn't retreat. "What happens after I flood your channel?"

"I put you on your knees so you can present your ass to me," Sawyer said. "I'll take my time and treat it so good. Maybe get you aroused again."

Chuckling, Royce raised his head and smirked at him. "Don't get comfortable down there. I nearly went off like a rocket the moment your dick touched mine. I'll probably cream your tight pucker before I'm halfway inside you."

Sawyer fisted Royce's hair and tugged him down for a passionate kiss. His husband's desperation only made Sawyer hornier, putting his flip-fuck fantasy at risk, especially when Royce started rocking his hips again. Sawyer tore his mouth free and said, "You're not the only one who's about to go off like a rocket. Okay, new plan."

Royce chuckled and covered his mouth with a finger. "No plan. Legs up, lube on, and we lose ourselves in the moment."

Sawyer pulled his legs back until his knees were nearly touching his shoulders, showing what role he wanted to take. "You can be the pillow princess next time."

Royce prepped, stretched, and notched his cock against Sawyer's hole. He kept his gray eyes locked on him as he pushed inside. Full lips parted on an exhale that was half sigh and half moan. "Been too long." Royce stopped halfway inside, his cock throbbing in time with Sawyer's racing heart. "Damn, I need this. I need you, baby."

"I'm right here. Take me."

Royce snapped his hips forward, burying himself deep. "Need you."

"Show me."

They moved together then, bodies gliding and hands roaming. Incredible sex was nothing new, but this felt…next-level. Sawyer crossed his ankles over Royce's firm ass and used his heels to spur him on, to plunge deeper and fuck harder. It still wasn't enough. The same desperation Sawyer had felt earlier surged higher, and he rolled Royce onto his back and straddled his hips. Royce's gray eyes darkened with the passionate tempest brewing inside, and Sawyer gave himself over to the maelstrom of emotions taking over his body. There was a world happening outside their bedroom door, but neither of them was aware of it. Sawyer found the perfect angle so that Royce's dick hit his prostate just right. He planted his palms on Royce's chest and rode him with reckless abandon.

Royce ghosted his fingertips over Sawyer's chest and rubbed his nipples with his thumbs. "So fucking sexy." His hand drifted lower until it brushed against Sawyer's bouncing cock. "Need me to jerk you off?"

Sawyer shook his head. His pleasure had built to a blinding crescendo. He was right there. Just needed one more. Right fucking there. His breath snagged in his throat as he came. His first spurt landed on Royce's chin and neck. "Oh fuck."

"That's it, baby." Royce gripped his hips and bounced him up and down his shaft. "Use me."

Sawyer rode out his orgasm until he had nothing left to give. Royce dug his heels into the mattress and thrust upward, shooting his release into Sawyer's tight channel.

"This is my favorite kind of mess to clean up," Sawyer said. He swiped his finger through the mess he'd made on Royce's face.

Grabbing Sawyer's wrist, Royce said, "Gimme?" He licked the finger clean and tugged Sawyer down for a deep kiss.

They lay snuggled together for several minutes before reality returned.

"Cleaning, huh?" Royce asked.

Sawyer laughed and rolled onto his back before they ended up stuck together. "Our house is a mess."

"Correction: our home looks like a family with a newborn lives here."

"I want to have family dinners again on Sundays with Dane and Cayden. I don't want them to feel displaced now that we have a baby."

"Yeah, I've thought about that too. I miss them."

"Me too," Sawyer said. "So, we tidy up a little and figure out which casserole we want to thaw out for Sunday."

"My vote is for the chicken and stuffing Jo made us. That's one of my favorites."

"We can serve it with mashed potatoes, some kind of vegetable, and rolls," Sawyer said. "We'll need to put a grocery order together."

"Uh-huh," Royce said around a yawn.

Sawyer turned his head and glared at Royce, not that he noticed Sawyer's ire with his eyes closed. "Don't go to sleep."

"I'm not. Just resting my eyes until my legs recover." Royce yawned again and reached for the covers shoved at the foot of the bed, where they'd left them at Darla o'clock that morning. "Might as well cover up."

"Your dick is slick with your orgasm, and my spunk is all over you."

Royce gave a halfhearted shrug and another yawn. "Can't be assed right now. Maybe we should take a power nap before we clean. Just thirty minutes."

"Fine. I'll set a timer so we don't sleep until dinner." Sawyer leaned over the bed, grabbed the first article of clothing he reached, and came up with a shirt. He mopped up most of the mess on both of them and tossed the shirt back onto the floor.

Royce covered them up and turned onto his side. Sawyer spooned in behind him and was out like a light until a ringing phone woke him up. He was disoriented at first because the room was darker than he'd expected after a little nap. That's when he realized he'd forgotten to set an alarm on his watch, and they'd slept much longer than they'd planned. With winter's shorter days, it was hard to judge the time, but he'd bet it was at least three o'clock.

Royce sat up suddenly beside him. "Oh shit. Where's the baby?"

"At my mom's." Sawyer threw back the covers and swung his legs out of bed. "That was probably her calling because she hasn't heard from us for so long."

"It's more likely your dad calling because he wants his wife back," Royce said, nestling deeper under the blanket.

Sawyer padded into the living room and checked his phone for missed calls. He didn't have any, so he tapped the screen on Royce's phone and froze at what he saw there. Ivy had called Royce twice, sent a text message, and left a voicemail. Sawyer stared at the screen until the phone went dark. He knew Royce's passcode and could access the messages, but he couldn't make himself move. He just stood there, frozen in place, as his mind conjured all the scary things she could've said.

A chill started in Sawyer's extremities and worked its way toward the center of his body, as if he'd been left out in the cold. And wasn't that the crux of his deepest fears? The one thing he wouldn't allow himself to voice, not even to himself. That he'd be left in the cold when the dust settled. Sawyer couldn't see a judge denying Royce custody of his daughter, but he could see a world that denied Sawyer's legal recognition as Darla's father. The chill crept into his chest and wrapped around his heart, squeezing until its beat became a slow, dull thud in his ears.

Left in the cold.

A rattling noise joined the thud. Were those his bones? Was he about to break apart at the seams? It took Sawyer a moment to realize the noise came from his chattering teeth.

"Sawyer." Royce's voice was close, and he sounded worried. "Baby, what's wrong? Is Darla okay?"

He fought through the freezing fear and met his husband's frightened gaze. "Lost in the cold."

"What do you mean? Who's lost in the cold?"

Sawyer shook his head. "I am."

Royce rubbed his hands up and down Sawyer's biceps. "I bet you are freezing. You're standing buck-ass naked in the living room in February."

The skin-on-skin friction sparked warmth and feeling into Sawyer's arms, but his mind remained paralyzed in fear. "Ivy called," he finally said.

Royce's hands stilled. "What did she say?"

"I don't know," Sawyer replied. "She only called you. I'm not Darla's father. I'm not her anything."

"Baby," Royce said. "Don't do this." He wrapped a throw blanket around Sawyer's shoulders and pulled him into his embrace. "We already know what Ivy is going to tell us. Our adoption hearing is going to be delayed. Could be weeks, or it could be months. But it will happen. I believe this with every bone in my body. I need you to believe it too."

"But if it doesn't—"

"No," Royce said. "We are not doing this to ourselves. Darla Grace

Locke is your daughter in every way that counts, and you will get the legal documents to prove it. Do you hear me?"

"But—"

Royce shook his head. "No buts. Do you trust me?" He took Sawyer's hands, stared him in the eyes, and slowly repeated the question. "Do you trust me?"

"With every fiber of my being." No hesitation or reservations. "You're my one true constant."

"We will move to another state if that's what it takes," Royce said. "Nothing and no one is going to keep you from the life I promised you."

Sawyer breathed deeply and silently repeated the vow, wrapping the beautiful words around his heart until he covered all the cracks. "I believe you."

"Good." Royce kissed him, letting his lips linger for a few seconds before pulling back. "Let's see what Ivy has to say." He released Sawyer to pick up his phone. "She texted around one o'clock just to say that she should have some news about our adoption this afternoon. She called twice just before we woke up and left a message." Royce clicked on the voicemail, and Ivy simply asked him to call back at his earliest convenience. He tapped the phone icon to dial her back and placed the call on speaker.

"Hello, Royce," Ivy said when she answered. Her voice was calm and neutral, so it was impossible to read anything into it.

"Sorry I missed your messages today."

"No worries. Life with a newborn can be chaotic."

"It is," Royce agreed. "Do you have an update about our adoption?"

"As I cautioned, Judge Hampton has temporarily postponed all adoptions being processed through our firm while they do a review of past cases involving the adoption agency at the center of the allegations."

"But we're not affiliated with Shania Price," Sawyer said.

"Hello, Sawyer," Ivy said. "While that's true, the judge is going to review some of our other cases at random just to ensure we're operating ethically. Guys, I know I have no right to ask this, but I need you to believe me when I say she will not find a smoking gun. Ned Owens lost his life because he was going to take this shady lady down. Every single lawyer working at our firm was adopted or has adopted children, so this is very personal for us. We know how important it is for things to be done properly. Your adoption will proceed in your favor. It's just a matter of time."

Sawyer released a shaky breath. "I can't imagine how stressful this entire situation is for the parents at the center of this nightmare. My heart goes out to them."

"Mine does as well," Royce said.

"Look, I can't go into great detail, but I want you to know that our agency is working on an arrangement that benefits both the adoptive families, the birth parents, and the innocent children caught in the middle. I've also referred the birth mothers to a litigator who will represent them pro bono. They will serve Shania Price with a civil lawsuit notice as soon as authorities locate her. A judge won't preside over a civil case until the criminal matters are resolved, but they'll freeze her assets so she can't sell off everything."

"That's good news," Sawyer said. "Thank you for sharing that with us."

"I have even better news," Ivy said. "Judge Hampton brought up your case specifically today. She's received all the documentation to proceed as soon as the audit is over. She made several complimentary remarks about you without provocation from me."

"Like what?" Royce asked.

"She told me that your home care specialist gave you rave reviews and that your adoption recommendation letters were some of the most touching she's read in three decades on the bench. You've got this, guys, and I can say it with my whole chest."

"Thank you, Ivy. Keep us posted on anything else you hear."

"You got it. Just keep loving your daughter and let me fret about the legal stuff."

"Will do." Royce disconnected the call and gripped the throw blanket to tug Sawyer closer. "Do you feel better?"

Sawyer did a quick body scan and didn't find any lingering tension. "Yes. Much better."

"Good. You look ridiculous." He slapped Sawyer's ass through the blanket. "Get dressed, and let's power clean for the next forty minutes so your mom won't know we fucked and slept all day long when we were supposed to clean."

Sawyer laughed. "She knows damn well what we've been up to. Hell, she encouraged it."

"Doesn't mean I want her to see the evidence," Royce said. "Where do you want to start?"

Sawyer eyed the fit of Royce's sweats again.

"Don't you dare look at me like that again. There's no time for oofing around. We have serious work to do."

Sawyer let the throw blanket fall to the floor and basked in the admiration flaring in Royce's eyes. "Fine," he said with a heavy sigh. "I'll go get dressed." He felt the heat of Royce's lustful gaze on his naked backside when he walked away and started a silent countdown. He'd made it to four before the sounds of Royce's hot pursuit reached his ears.

Fight, flight, or oof? Was there any question? Sawyer sprinted down the hallway, knowing the fun that awaited him. First the flight, then the oof.

CHAPTER ELEVEN

ROYCE SLID HIS ARM AROUND SAWYER'S WAIST AND LOOKED down at the pizza box sporting a Savannah bakery logo that promised the world's best brookies. "What exactly is a brookie? And who decided this bakery makes the best?"

Sawyer opened the lid and revealed a massive chocolate chip cookie and brownie hybrid that smelled like heaven. "This is a brookie." He leaned forward and sniffed. "I just gained five pounds." He shook his head and closed the lid. "We shouldn't serve this."

"You're right. We just fed them a feast," he said, nodding toward the living room, where their family gathered. "They shouldn't expect dessert from two men with a three-week-old baby."

Sawyer turned to him and rolled his eyes. "Not for that reason."

"You don't need to watch your weight," Royce protested. "You've already resumed your workouts, and I read that feeding a baby burns off a lot of calories."

"Breastfeeding burns calories. Neither of us is producing milk."

Royce pursed his lips in confusion. "Then why can't we eat the crownie?"

"Brookie."

"Same difference," Royce said. "They both mean the same thing."

"Brookie sounds cuter. Crownie is too clown-y."

Royce quirked his brow. "Is this the beginning of corny dad jokes and puns?"

Smiling, Sawyer said, "I guess it could be."

"So, why can't we eat the dessert you bought?"

"That's the thing," Sawyer said. "I didn't buy it. Alec sent it as a gift, but Dane is the actual intended recipient because it's his favorite."

"Why didn't he send it directly to him, then? Cayden told me Alec and Dane talk all the time."

"Yes, but Alec is trying to give Dane the space he needs to heal. He thought sending the brookie might come across as a romantic gesture."

"Because it is," Royce said. "Dane will get heart eyes when he sees it. Mark my words."

"Not if he doesn't know it's from Alec," Sawyer countered. "We're supposed to serve it to everyone without mentioning where it came from."

"Alec doesn't want credit?" Royce asked.

"Nope. He just wants to make Dane smile."

Royce pondered that for a minute. "Does Alec realize he's in love with Dane?"

"He does."

"And he plans to do something about it?" Royce asked.

"He does."

Royce sighed in frustration. "Anytime soon?"

"Alec will make his move when the time is right," Sawyer said. "And before you ask, I don't know when that will be. They both have a lot of healing to do, and Alec is constantly traveling for his podcast production."

"Love will find a way," Royce said.

A collective "aww" came from the living room, and the guys turned in that direction. Kelsey was burping Darla, and all heads had turned in their direction.

"Darla better not have given them her first smile," Sawyer said.

Eddie was the first to look toward the kitchen. "Your daughter belches like a drunken sailor."

Sawyer sighed in relief and whispered, "Oh, thank goodness."

"Wait until you hear her fart," Royce told his dad.

As if on cue, Darla let one rip, and the gathering said, "Awww," again.

"Dang, we heard that in here," Sawyer said.

"She gets that from the Locke side," Kelsey declared as she repositioned Darla to drink the second half of her bottle. When Andrew only cleared his throat, Kels turned her head and glared at him. "I dare you."

"What?" Andrew tapped his throat. "I just had a little tickle."

Ella, who sat in his lap, giggled and clapped her hands. "Me. Me. Ickle me."

"Tickle me," Kelsey said, emphasizing the *T*.

"In about three more weeks, dear," Andrew promised his wife. He dodged the burp rag she tossed at him, then wiggled his finger against Ella's collarbone to make her squeal in delight.

Royce turned his attention back to his husband and the delicious issue at hand. "Do we have something else we can offer for dessert? Then we can pretend to remember the brookie as we say good night to everyone and make it look like Dane would be doing us a big favor if he took it off our hands."

Sawyer grimaced. "I have all the sundae toppings I ordered from the grocery store to go on top of this."

Royce's eyes glazed over. "We're having brookie sundaes?"

"That was my goal. Do you think we could get by with just sundaes?" Sawyer snapped his fingers to get Royce's attention. "Did you hear my question?"

"I'm not sure I even know my name right now. All I can think of is building a massive sundae on top of that brookie." He shook his head to clear the image. "What kind of ice cream?" Nope. Still there.

Sawyer groaned as he headed to the refrigerator. He opened the freezer drawer and said, "You answered my question."

"I did? Because I'm pretty sure I blacked out."

"That was my answer."

Royce moved to Sawyer's side and gasped when he saw the six half gallons he'd selected. "I think we should just kick them all out now and live off brookie sundaes until there's nothing left."

"Tempting, but no."

"Okay, okay." Royce reached down and grabbed the mint chocolate chip and peanut butter chip. "This is a celebration dinner, and we should cap it off with a dessert equal to or greater than the food from the previous course."

"Does that rule come from the *Royce Locke Book of Entertaining?*" Sawyer set down the cherry cordial, vanilla bean, and strawberry ice cream cartons on the island, leaving fudge swirl for Royce to retrieve.

"No," he replied. "I'm trying to find a reason not to lick the brookie and yell 'mine' at the top of my lungs."

Sawyer growled playfully and tugged Royce into a hug. "I love being on the receiving end of those possessive licks."

"Yeah?" Royce maneuvered his husband a few feet to the right, shielding them from prying eyes in the living room. He nuzzled his nose against Sawyer's neck before licking a path up to his ear. "Mine."

Sawyer shivered hard, and his dark eyes glittered with arousal. "Lower next time."

"All the more reason to boot these people out of our house." Royce stepped back to put some room between them before things got out of hand. "What else do we need to lay out?"

Sawyer tipped his head toward the walk-in pantry. "The rest of the supplies are in here. Wanna help?"

Royce's pulse kicked up a notch. "For real, or is this a ploy to get me to yourself?"

"Yes."

They ducked into the pantry and shut the door. Royce backed Sawyer up against the nearest shelf and feasted on his mouth. Who needed fancy foods and desserts when he could have this? He tangled one hand in Sawyer's hair, angling his head to deepen the kiss. Sawyer slid both hands under Royce's sweater and slid them upward to caress his back.

Royce tore his mouth free and whispered, "I could drop to my knees and claim you now."

Sawyer was seconds away from telling him to do it when someone rapped on the pantry door.

"Um, guys," Eddie said from the other side. "Do you want us to head on out?"

"No," Sawyer said as Royce replied, "Yes."

Sawyer playfully pinched Royce to make him behave. "We're just getting out the rest of the ingredients for the sundaes."

"Uh-huh," Eddie said. "Didn't mean to interrupt the hunting and gathering. Carry on."

They waited until his footsteps faded before breaking into unhinged laughter.

"What's happened to us?" Royce asked. "Sneaking into our pantry for a quick fumble with a house full of people. For shame, for shame."

Sawyer waggled his brows. "Hot as hell though."

"We should role-play this when we're alone."

"Deal." Sawyer kissed him once more before turning to pull items off the shelf. He pulled the bottom of his shirt out to act as a pouch and chucked three different nuts, multiple flavored syrups, and a variety of sprinkles. "Will you grab the whipped cream and the container with fruit from the refrigerator?"

"Sure." Royce retrieved the items and helped Sawyer organize a brookie sundae bar on the island.

"I forgot to grab the paper bowls from the pantry."

"I'll grab them." Royce turned and walked backward. "Want to help?"

Sawyer inhaled slowly. "I'd better stay right here."

"Smart." Royce retrieved the bowls from the pantry and set them on the island. "This is quite a spread. I'd like to thank the people who invented the modern grocery delivery systems with—"

"Careful," Sawyer cautioned.

"—a friendly handshake."

Sawyer nodded his approval. "Let's call them all in for dessert."

"Yeah. Then they can go home, and I can possessively lick you all over."

Sawyer moaned softly before tearing himself away and walking toward the living room. "Dessert is ready."

Their guests didn't exactly stampede into the kitchen, but they moved with purpose. The Sutton brothers led the charge, which meant they had a front-row seat to Dane's reaction, and it didn't disappoint.

"A brookie!" Dane's face lit up with joy. "They're my favorite. I need to take a quick picture. Alec has never had one of these. I keep telling him we'll share one when he gets back to town."

Beside him, Sawyer snapped a discreet photo. Royce knew he'd send it to Alec later.

"Dude," Cayden said. "Don't worry about angles and lighting. You're not a foodie influencer on Insta. And don't drool on the brookie. The rest of us want some too."

Sawyer chuckled as he typed furiously on his phone. He hit Send and tucked his device away without Dane noticing. "Let's make sure Dane takes home the leftovers."

"Fine," Royce grumbled. "We're keeping the ice cream."

Evangeline and Jo *oohed* and *aahed* when they stepped up to the sundae bar and perused the options. The overhead lights caught the diamond solitaire on Jo's left ring finger.

Eddie, you sly dog. Royce didn't draw attention to it since the engaged couple hadn't announced the news, but he'd mention it to his father when he could talk to him alone.

"Nice spread," Jace said as he piled three different scoops of ice cream on his slice of brookie. He looked over his shoulder at Holly, who was carrying Harper on her hip. "Want me to make one for you?" Jace asked her.

Holly made a weird noise, turned an awful shade of green, and thrust Harper into his arms before bolting from the room. Jace grimaced as his wife left, then turned to Royce. "Do you have any saltines?"

Royce retrieved a sleeve from the pantry and handed them to his brother. "Does this mean what I think it does?"

Jace smiled impishly. "She's hit that rough patch in the first trimester."

"Congratulations," Royce said, hugging Jace and Harper. "I'm so happy for you."

"Thanks. I'll be even happier when Holly feels better. If this pregnancy is like Harper's, that should happen in about two weeks." He tucked the sleeve of crackers under his arm, picked up his sundae, and went to find a place to sit down.

Eddie worried his bottom lip between his teeth when he stepped up to the sundae bar. "Probably should stick to the fruit with a little whipped cream."

"I almost forgot," Sawyer said. "I got something special for you, Eddie." He retrieved a special carton of ice cream that better aligned with his dietary needs.

Eddie smiled down at the thoughtful gesture. "You're a damn good son."

"Thank you."

"Don't suppose you have a low-carb, low-fat cookie thing somewhere?" Eddie asked.

"No, but I plan to cut off a small sliver of the brookie and crumble it on top of my sundae."

"Perfect idea," Eddie said. "I'll do the same thing."

"And I'll eat enough for all three of us," Royce said.

Eddie aimed a fork at him. "Better watch yourself, or you'll end up like me."

Once upon a time, those words would've triggered a host of negative reactions for Royce, but now they only made him smile. "A sexy silver fox with lethal charm? I'll take my chances."

Eddie guffawed and moved down the line.

Andrew, Kelsey, and Ella stepped up to make their sundaes next. Ella pointed at the goodies she wanted and clapped when her parents obeyed her commands. Father and daughter moved on down the line, but Kelsey joined them instead of making a sundae for herself.

"Your little miss will probably need a diaper change now that her formula has settled." She moved closer and lowered her voice. "Pretty sure one of those farts wasn't dry."

Sawyer cackled, kissed her cheek, and headed into the living room to get Darla from her bouncy chair.

"How's he really doing with the adoption delay?" Kelsey asked Royce once they were alone. "This must be especially hard for him. You and I know this is going to work out, but our rights aren't in question."

"I think the anticipation of the delay was almost harder than finally receiving the news. The buildup got to him, and he had some really dark moments where he wondered if he'd ever get to claim Darla as his legal daughter. We've had some heartfelt conversations over the past few days, and we're both in a good place. Having you here tonight helped, and I'm so glad you came. You should've brought your mom too."

Kelsey laughed. "She needed a break from us. She mentioned something about a bubble bath and excellent wine."

"How much longer is she staying?"

"Just one more week," Kelsey replied. "You can see I'm getting around well. I still have three more weeks before I can drive, but that's not really an issue. I don't have anywhere to be, and Andrew has plenty of saved personal time if I need him."

"Sawyer or I would happily chauffeur you around."

"Appreciate it." Ella called for her across the room, so she patted Royce's shoulder and headed that way.

He saw an opening at the brookie sundae and took it. He sliced a modest piece of the dessert and placed it at the bottom of the bowl. Royce topped it with a single scoop of peanut butter chip ice cream, chocolate sauce, a generous swirl of whipped cream, and a sprinkling of chopped peanuts. He stood off to the side of the room to eat his treat while watching Sawyer's interactions with Darla as he placed her back in her bouncy chair after her diaper change. Eddie tossed his bowl in the trash and joined him.

"I brought the letters from your Aunt Tipsy," he said. "I'll get them out of the car before we leave."

"Thank you." Royce had always loved Aunt Tipsy's handwriting. His favorite recipe cards were the ones she filled with her looping cursive. Royce had laminated them years ago to preserve those cherished pieces of the woman he loved so much. He chuckled when he imagined the gruff and gritty words she'd written to Eddie in her feminine script. Maybe Royce's expression gave the direction of his thoughts away because Eddie snorted.

"Yep. Some of those letters are as raucous as you're thinking. They practically singed my fingers when I held them."

"I bet. Aunt Tipsy was never one to hold back her opinion."

"The world had better look out if her namesake is half as feisty," Eddie said.

"So, I noticed something sparkly on Jo's ring finger. Why didn't you tell me you got engaged?"

Eddie's cheeks turned pink. "Tonight is about celebrating your new family, and we didn't want to pull focus. I'll shout it from the rooftops soon."

"Forget that," Royce said and cleared his throat obnoxiously loud. "There's more to celebrate tonight than our little angel." He looked at his dad with a raised brow.

Eddie grinned like an idiot as he sought Jo in the crowd. "My lady has agreed to marry me."

The room erupted in cheers as everyone moved to congratulate the engaged couple. Royce saluted Eddie with a spoonful of sundae and stepped out of the fray.

The gathering wound down after dessert. Dane didn't put up a fuss when Sawyer suggested he take the leftover brookie home, but he got really stubborn when Royce offered to help with upcoming expenses so he wouldn't have to work so much overtime.

"I admire your determination and independence," Royce said, "but don't let your positive traits become detrimental out of misguided stubbornness."

"I won't," Dane promised. "I have this under control."

"And if you discover otherwise?" Sawyer asked.

"I will call you. I promise." Dane hugged them both and headed outside to where Cayden waited in the car. The teenager had talked nonstop about his driver's education classes and the practice driving they'd been doing. Cayden waved from behind the steering wheel, and the dashboard illuminated his excited face. Dane stopped and faced them. "If you want to help, you could ride shotgun with Cayden a few times a week to help him get more driving experience."

Royce sensed a potential trap, but he stepped into it anyway. "Of course. Just let me know when."

"You got it."

Dane got in the car and barely had time to buckle up before Cayden backed down the driveway without looking in either direction. They lived in a quiet residential neighborhood, but they had occasional traffic, and this was one of those times.

"Watch out," Royce hollered from the porch, even though they couldn't hear him.

Cayden slammed on the brakes, and the oncoming car swerved and nearly ran up on the curb to miss him. The teenager beeped and waved his apology before driving off. Dane clutched his chest with one hand and a chunk of brookie in the other.

"Oh fuck," Royce said after Cayden drove out of sight. "I'm in for it."

"There's no way in hell you're getting me in that death trap," Sawyer said. He patted Royce on the shoulder and walked inside the house. "You're on your own, baby."

"Thanks."

The rest of their guests filed out, hugging or kissing them good-bye. Eddie walked Jo to the car and retrieved the letters. "I kept the pictures of you kids and the artwork y'all made. These are just letters." The box was larger than Royce had expected.

"She must've liked you more than I realized."

"Nah," Eddie said. "Everything she did was for you kids. She would've done anything to make me a better man because it would've made me a better dad. I really wish your mama and Aunt Tipsy were here to see how I've turned out. Finally."

Royce looked up at the twinkling stars in the velvety midnight blue sky. "Who's to say they don't have a front-row seat?"

"I'd like to believe it," Eddie said as he pulled Royce into a hug. "Tell my granddaughter that Poppy loves her and will be back soon. I had to share her with too many people tonight."

"I will."

Royce waved as Eddie backed down the driveway, then went back inside the house. He carried the box into the living room and set it on the coffee table.

"Oh, what's that?"

"The letters Aunt Tipsy sent to Eddie while he was in prison," Royce replied.

"I bet you're dying to dig in."

"Maybe a little," Royce admitted. "But it can wait until after I help you tidy up."

"Evangeline and Jo restored order before they left."

"Moms are always several steps ahead of us mere mortals," Royce said.

"Always. Is it okay if I read them with you?"

"Of course."

Sawyer scooted next to Royce and looped his arm around his lower back.

Royce reached into the box and pulled out a short stack of letters. His heart expanded just from seeing Tipsy's handwriting on the outside of the envelope. He took a moment to trace the loops and curves before pulling out the first letter. "Oh wow. This probably arrived during Eddie's first week in prison." He unfolded the letter and snorted at what he read.

Dear Edward,

How an insufferable dipshit like you produced these beautiful children is beyond me. They're adjusting well, and so am I. Last week, you said something after your sentencing that has stuck with me. You said that you owe me for stepping in. And you're right. You do, and I'm calling in my chips. From this day forward, get your shit together. Be the man these precious kids deserve. I'll keep writing and sending updates in case you deserve them someday. If not, you're only hurting yourself. Now, how do I sign off a letter to someone I can barely tolerate? I'll keep trying something new until I find the perfect fit.

Fuck you,
Tipsy

"Wow," Sawyer said. "I want to be like her when I grow up."

Royce set the letter down and chose the next in the stack. It must've been one that included pictures, because Aunt Tipsy had only written the date and location, which was the Fourth of July parade. She signed off with the same fuck you at the bottom. "Guess she hit pay dirt on her first attempt."

"I will be curious to see how the tone changed over time. But not right now. Tonight is a special occasion." When Sawyer only arched a brow, Royce said, "Darla's umbilical cord fell off, and she gets a proper bath."

"You want to do that now?"

Royce nodded. "I can't wait to see how she reacts."

They both looked at the bouncy chair to find their daughter wide-awake.

Sawyer jumped up from the couch. "I'll grab the tub and bath caddy. You get Darla and meet me in the kitchen."

Royce grinned at their daughter as he unbuckled her from the chair. He held her against his chest, kissed the top of her head, and headed into the kitchen. They would turn the island into a baby spa until she was old enough to sit upright in the bathtub chair. Sawyer arrived a few minutes later, pushing the three-tiered bath cart that held everything they needed to pamper their Lil Pumpkin.

"One of us has to document this big moment with pictures and videos," Sawyer said. "We'll cover up her little bits with washcloths and focus on her face."

"I'll be the photographer, and you be the mean guy who puts her in water."

Sawyer smiled at him. "Or the hero who starts her out on a life-long journey of quality self-care." He fussed with the water, trying to achieve the perfect temperature. He put the floating duck in the portable bath and judged the numbers, adding a little cold or a little hot until he had it just right. "Hand me our darling."

Royce had stripped her down to her diaper and wrapped her in a towel to keep her warm while they waited. Sawyer placed her on the changing pad to remove her diaper and clean her with a wipe before easing her into the water.

She gasped a little, scrunched up her face, and opened her mouth like she might cry, until he submerged her butt all the way into the tub. The water barely came up to her belly button, but she let out a little sigh of contentment.

"Are you catching these expressions?" Sawyer asked.

"Every single one."

Sawyer gently wet her hair and worked shampoo into her curls. Then he switched to a round silicone thing to massage her scalp. "My Lil Pumpkin loves having her hair washed," he cooed. "Isn't that right, sweetheart?"

Darla looked up at him and smiled.

Sawyer stilled and swung his wide-eyed gaze at Royce. "Did you see that?"

"Sure did."

"Did you capture it?"

"Yeah, and I'm still rolling."

"I got her first smile," Sawyer said as he shimmied.

"I mean, I'm standing right here too."

Sawyer turned his attention back to Darla. "It was all for me, wasn't it, baby girl?" And the little heart snatcher smiled again. Sawyer fist-pumped the air and shimmied some more, making Royce eternally grateful he hadn't stopped filming yet. Sawyer glanced at him again, this time with tears in his eyes. "She loves me so much."

Royce clicked the red circle to cut the video. He leaned in and kissed Sawyer before smiling down at Darla. "Of course she loves you. She loves me too, right, angel?" Her mouth moved, but she didn't smile. "I'll win you over yet."

"Can you hand me the baby wash? I want to use the purple bottle. It's supposed to help her sleep."

Royce walked to the other side of the island, tripped over the cat, and cursed a blue streak before remembering his audience.

"She smiled again!" Sawyer exclaimed.

Royce stared down at Darla, who suddenly looked serious. "You think it's funny when Papa does stupid things? Or was it his salty language?"

"I think both," Sawyer said.

They carefully washed her before the water cooled, then wrapped her in one of those towels with the cute head pocket. This one made her look like a tiny frog, and Royce snapped several pictures. Once she was dry, they put a diaper on her and a pair of super-soft pajamas with little bunnies all over them. The big event had made her sleepy, and she conked out against Sawyer's chest. She looked so tiny, and Sawyer seemed so peaceful. Royce snapped several more photos before an idea occurred to him.

"I want to start a new kitchen tradition," Royce announced as he thumbed through his music app. He found Adele's cover of "Make You Feel My Love" and pushed Play. He opened his arms, and Sawyer smiled as he stepped into his embrace. They danced slowly, forehead to forehead, while their Lil Pumpkin slept peacefully between them. This moment with their daughter was so damn perfect, he wished he could hold on to it forever.

"The two of you are all I'll ever need," Royce told them.

Darla's lips curved up into a smile, and a dimple winked in her cheek.

"Yes," Royce whispered. "She might be asleep, but it still counts. She's crazy about me too."

"No one can resist that Locke charm."

CHAPTER TWELVE

A DELIVERY UPDATE NOTIFICATION POPPED UP ON SAWYER'S phone that made him deliriously happy. "Derrick has my package, and I'm next in line to receive my delivery."

Royce dropped the remote on the coffee table and aimed a menacing look in his direction. "Excuse me? This sounds an awful lot like a porn setup."

Sawyer shimmied his shoulders and waggled his brows. "Derrick does sound like the name of a porn star with a massive package."

Royce turned his body toward him. "Explain yourself before I get really jealous and probably pissed too."

"Language, my love," Sawyer crooned.

Royce jabbed his finger toward the baby monitor on the coffee table and said, "Our daughter is sleeping in her bassinet in our bedroom with her guard cat on duty. She's six weeks old and couldn't repeat the word even if she'd heard it. Pissed, pissed, pissed. That's what I'm going to be if this Derrick shows up and whips out a massive schlong."

Sawyer tackled Royce onto the couch and straddled his hips. "Don't be mad, baby. I'll let you watch."

"I'll go to prison," Royce declared. "I mean it."

"Your schlong is the only one I want." Sawyer cupped Royce's face with both hands and kissed him, but he kept his mouth firmly closed in protest. "I don't know jack about Derrick other than he works for FedEx."

"And has a massive package to del—"

Sawyer cut him off with a hard kiss. "It's a custom gift I ordered right after we confirmed Kelsey's pregnancy. It's something I saw on Etsy and had to have, even though there was a long waiting list."

Royce glanced over at the monitor, confirmed Darla was still sleeping, and kissed a trail along Sawyer's neck. "Our buddy Derrick can drop the box on the porch and get out of here." He gripped Sawyer's ass with both hands and thrust his hips upward. "I've got your package right here."

Sawyer snickered. "I can't take you seriously when you break out the cheesy porn lines."

"Really?" Royce nipped that sensitive spot just below Sawyer's ear and sent a delicious shiver down his spine. "How about now?"

"Meh."

Royce's dark chuckle rumbled against Sawyer's flesh, and his pucker flexed in anticipation of the hell he was about to pay. Royce slid a hand under his waistband and pressed a finger against his entrance. "Liar," he whispered. "I feel how badly you want me. I can make you forget all about your custom…whatever."

Sawyer's breath quickened, and his hips canted toward Royce's erection of their own volition, proving his husband correct. "The package isn't for me though. It's for you."

Royce put both hands on Sawyer's chest and shoved playfully.

"Well, why didn't you say so?" He sat up and straightened his clothes and hair. "How do I look?" He snagged Sawyer's phone off the coffee table. "If the notification tells you his name, does it also show you a picture?"

"Yep."

"Whoa!" Royce turned the phone around to show a smiling Black man who looked too much like Shemar Moore for Sawyer's comfort. "I bet Derrick gives new meaning to daddy."

Sawyer snatched his phone with a huff and tucked it into his pocket. "I bought something really special for you to share with your daughter, and you're going to ruin the surprise with tawdry remarks."

Royce immediately sobered up. "I'm sorry." He leaned forward to kiss Sawyer lightly on the mouth. "Take off your clothes, and I'll make it up to you."

Sawyer huffed a put-upon sigh. "I'd let you try, but my gift is so generous that I have to sign for it."

Arching a brow, Royce said, "I didn't even have to sign for my new iPhone. They just left that fucker on the front porch. What did you buy?"

"Amy from the Daisy Patch cares more about us than our phone carrier does."

"Unless we don't pay our bill," Royce said. "Then they'd care a whole lot."

"True."

Royce bounced a little on the sofa cushion. "What did you get us?"

"It won't be a surprise if I tell you," Sawyer said. "Derrick will be here soon, and you can open it."

"When did FedEx start this detailed service? When I order something, I just get a window of delivery time."

"I think I signed up for package management or something. Or maybe it's because I have to sign for the delivery. Does it matter? They're not running a dating app."

"Not so sure when they hire drivers that look like that." Royce waggled his brows. "And we get to meet that hunk."

"Don't embarrass us," Sawyer pleaded.

Royce tilted his head to the side and pursed his lips. "Do you think FedEx has a hunky delivery guy calendar? What month would Derrick be? August because it's smoking hot, and so is he."

Sawyer tapped his fingers on his knee. "Are you finished?"

Smiling wickedly, Royce looked down at his crotch. "I think I'm just getting started."

"That's it." Sawyer took him back down to the couch, but they rolled and crashed hard on the rug. The air whooshed out of them with a double *oof*, and they laughed as soon as they could breathe again. "You are so ridiculous."

Royce cupped Sawyer's face and stared into his eyes. Derrick, his package, and even the world all faded away. "Yes, but you love me."

"So damn much."

They both leaned in for a kiss at the same time, their gestures routine, even if their emotions were anything but. Royce slid a hand under his shirt, and Sawyer rocked his hips, looking to pick up where they'd left off. Both their phones emitted the Ring chime to indicate motion detection in the driveway. They'd disconnected their regular doorbell a few weeks ago when the sound of it triggered an unholy chain of chaos that nobody needed. Royce had gone above and beyond installing a simple Ring doorbell though. He'd placed security systems to monitor every entrance, but Sawyer put his foot down when it came to adding interior monitoring, comparing it to living in the *Big Brother* house. Royce hadn't known what that was, and Sawyer wanted to prevent another reality show addiction, so he'd compromised and allowed Royce to put a floodlight near the peak of the garage roof. That was the one that had alerted them to driveway activity.

Royce reached for his phone on the coffee table and played the camera feed. "Let's go sign for the package so we can get back to this."

Sawyer rolled off him and stood up. He extended a hand to Royce and tugged him to his feet. "Better not open your surprise, or you'll forget all about me."

Royce looked back down at his phone. "Whoa!"

"Yeah, we know Derrick is hot."

"Well, yeah," Royce said, "but I'm talking about his package. That thing is huge."

Sawyer snatched the phone from his hand in time to see Derrick wheeling a large box toward the porch. He went to give the phone back to his husband, but Royce was already halfway to the front door. "Get back here, you shit!" Sawyer tossed the phone onto the sofa and jogged after him.

Dolly, who hadn't yet learned what the Ring chimes meant, reacted to her dads' energy, yipping and chasing after them.

Royce reached the door first, but Sawyer body-slammed him against it before he could open it. The doorbell chime went off on their phones in the living room as they wrestled over the doorknob. Derrick had to be wondering what the grunting and thumping was all about. Dolly's loud bark cut through their tomfoolery, and Sawyer picked the dog up to quiet her.

"Yes!" Royce cheered in victory before he wrenched the door open and startled the oh-so beautiful deliveryman. He propped his arm on the doorjamb and said, "Hello there."

"Hi." Derrick's lips curved into a delicious smile. "I have a package for Sawyer Locke."

"And what a mighty big pack—"

Sawyer threw an elbow, cutting Royce off and muscling his way to the door. "That's me. I'm Sawyer Locke."

Royce rubbed his chest and glared at Sawyer. "Asshole," he grumbled.

"Dickhead," Sawyer fired back.

"Um," Derrick said with a chuckle. "One of you needs to sign my ePod for this delivery."

"I'll do it." Royce turned to Sawyer. "You're holding Dolly."

The dog reacted to her name by wriggling and letting out an excited yip. Or maybe she thought Derrick was handsome too; either way, she got the man's attention.

He smiled at Dolly and said, "Oh, aren't you the prettiest thing."

"Thanks," Sawyer said. "That was from Dolly. You weren't calling me pretty."

"I could hold her while you sign," Derrick said, smiling at Sawyer. "I love dogs, but my boyfriend is allergic."

Dolly yipped again and wriggled harder when Derrick set his ePod on top of the box and reached for her.

"The dude needs to go," Royce announced.

Derrick's hands stilled. "My boyfriend? We've been together for five years, and he's not allergic to all animals."

"No," Royce said with a firm head shake. "You, buddy." He picked up the ePod and stylus from the box and scrawled his name on the screen. "First you charm my man, and now you're after my dog?"

"Don't listen to him," Sawyer said, extending Dolly toward Derrick with a smug expression.

Derrick cuddled the dog and talked to her in the sweetest voice. Dolly made a real slut of herself, licking his face and wriggling against his big, muscular chest.

"Would you like something to drink, Derrick?" Sawyer asked. "It's awfully hot out there."

"It's sixty degrees," Royce snarled. "He's fine."

Derrick raised his head and smiled. "I am fine, but thank you."

Royce must've reached his breaking point, declaring, "That's enough," as he took their dog back. "Good day to you, sir."

Derrick winked at Sawyer and blew a kiss at Dolly. "Have a great weekend, fellas." He grabbed his two-wheeled cart and whistled as he returned to his truck.

Royce glowered until Derrick pulled out of their driveway. He handed Dolly to Sawyer and scooted the big box into the foyer. "What the heck is in here?"

"You won't believe it," Sawyer said.

"Seems like this is the morning for incomprehensible things." Royce shut the door and faced Sawyer with hands on hips. "Shameful."

"What did I do?" Sawyer asked.

"I was talking to Dolly, but you're in the doghouse too."

"I repeat, 'What did I do?'"

Royce batted his eyelashes frantically and infused as much husk into his voice when he said, "Would you like something to drink, Derrick? It's awfully…hot out there."

Sawyer slumped against the closed door and laughed at his outlandish portrayal. "I didn't sound like that, and stop batting your eyelashes. It looks like you've developed a painful nervous tic." Sawyer straightened to his full height and pointed at Royce. "And you're one to talk."

"Me? I simply greeted the man when I opened the door."

Sawyer pursed his lips and leaned against the door to mirror Royce's earlier pose. "Hello there, big boy."

Snorting, Royce shook his head. "I didn't say that."

"And you were going to mention his mighty big package before I cut you off." Sawyer rolled his eyes. "Seriously, save your outrage."

"It is a huge package," Royce said, gesturing to the box in the foyer. He rubbed his hands together excitedly. "Can I open it? Can I?"

"We should probably wait for Eddie. He will get the biggest kick out of it."

Royce huffed and pouted like a toddler. "But I've already had to wait for months."

"You didn't know the gift existed until twenty minutes ago."

Stomping his foot, Royce said, "And it's been the longest twenty minutes of my life."

"Fine. Let me help you push it into the living room. I don't want you to reinjure your hamstring. There are things I want to do with you." He looked at his watch. "And Darla should sleep for at least another half hour. We can pack a lot of pleasure in that amount of time."

Royce stepped closer until the only thing separating them was Dolly. "Does it involve me ringing your bell, getting out my schlong, and delivering a package?"

"Mm-hmm," Sawyer said. He moved in closer to kiss Royce, but Dolly beat him to it. "But you'll have to wipe your mouth first."

Sawyer took Dolly back to the sofa and waited while Royce retrieved their two-wheeled cart from the garage. He moved the box to the living room and whipped out a box cutter.

"Be careful."

Royce sighed and shook his head. "I won't ruin my gift." He made shallow cuts across the top to reveal a slab of Styrofoam. "Baby, you shouldn't have."

"You won't be laughing when you see what's tucked inside there," Sawyer boasted.

"It's that good, huh?"

"Oh yeah."

Royce lifted off the top slab of Styrofoam, and a sheet of paper fell to the floor. "Probably the packing list."

"Don't look at it," Sawyer said. "It will spoil the surprise." He reached down for the paper when his phone rang. Charlie's name appeared on the screen, and he grabbed the phone instead. His pulse kicked up a notch every time his friend called with an update, but he'd stopped thinking "this is it" weeks ago to preserve his sanity. "Hey, Charlie."

"Is Royce close by? I'm about to hold a press conference and don't have much time to talk."

"Yeah, he's here." Sawyer's heartbeat kicked into a full gallop as he tapped the speakerphone icon.

Royce's head snapped up, and hopeful eyes locked on Sawyer. "Hi, Charlie. What's up?"

"We got them! Peyton and Shania Price and Landen Jordan are in police custody in New Mexico. US Marshals are en route to pick them up and bring them back to Georgia. I'm about to announce the arrests in a press conference, but I wanted you to hear the news from me first."

"Thank you so much," Sawyer said. "This means the world to us."

"We owe you one," Royce added.

"No, you don't. But I'd like to get together soon so I can meet your little girl."

"Let us know when you're free," Sawyer told him. "We're always home."

Charlie chuckled. "Will do." Muffled voices came from his end of the conversation. "Gotta run, guys. I'll be in touch soon." He clicked off before either of them could say goodbye.

"Do you want to see if the local news carries the press conference?" Royce asked.

"Nope," Sawyer said. "I'm content just knowing they've been arrested."

"It won't help our situation, but I feel relieved they won't escape justice." Royce reached for his hand and kissed the back of it. "And we're going to have a completely different day in court, with a much better outcome than those psychopaths. I believe that with my whole heart."

"Me too." Sawyer nodded toward the box. "Now, unpack your surprise. I'm dying to see what you think."

Royce reached inside the box and pulled out a pink plastic drill. A broad smile spread across his face. "Battery operated?"

"Yes, but I have to buy those separately. It has little fake drill bits somewhere in the box."

Royce squeezed the trigger and made the whirring noises himself. Dolly yipped from the couch and wagged her tail. "This isn't for you. It says Darla's name right on the side." He tapped the white lettering before letting the dog sniff it. Dolly wasn't impressed and lowered her head between her paws in a pout. "What else do we have in here?"

"Unpack it and see."

Royce pulled out a wrench, a tiny hammer, and several little tools. Then he started pulling out bigger wooden pieces that he'd have to assemble. There was a pegboard to hang her little tools and the work apron with her name embroidered on it. There was the workbench that Royce would attach her vise and saw to, and the storage area beneath it to store the wooden toolbox. He took his time unwrapping each piece, his expression getting sappier with every reveal. "You know she can't play with this for a long time."

"Yes, but you can assemble it and put it in her room because it's so stinking cute. Some princesses drink tea with their daddies, and others pretend to build stuff."

Royce looked up from the assembly instructions for the workbench. "I'll drink tea too. I'll wear a tutu, a tiara, or anything else my baby girl wants. Hell, the Rock lets his little girls put makeup on him. Nothing is off-limits for my Darla."

"I know, and I love you for it."

"This is an amazing gift. Thank you."

"You're welcome." Sawyer picked up the adorable canvas apron and said, "This is even better quality than I expected. So worth the long wait."

Royce cocked his head to the side. "When did you order this?"

"As soon as Kelsey confirmed her pregnancy," Sawyer said as he inspected the little hammer. "The waitlist was insane."

Royce picked up the packing list off the floor, read it, and then looked at Sawyer through narrowed eyes.

"Yes, it was pricey. But look at the quality."

"I'm not concerned about the cost," Royce said, pointing at the order date.

"I told you I ordered it a long time ago. Maybe it was silly to customize it the way I did, but we knew in our hearts that we were having a girl. We'd already chosen to name a daughter after your Aunt Tipsy. And it didn't really feel like a gamble with such a long wait time. I could've emailed the seller if we'd found out we were having a boy."

"Uh-huh," Royce said. "All of that's true."

"Then why am I getting the gunslinger glare?"

"Because you customized the workbench and tools with Darla's name on them three months before I told you my Aunt Tipsy's name."

Sawyer grinned sheepishly. "Oh yeah. About that…"

"You already knew," Royce said flatly.

"Funny story."

"I'll be the judge of that." Royce set the packing list aside and stalked toward him on his knees. "I can't believe you let me boast about knowing something you didn't."

"You were having so much fun." Sawyer scooted toward the end of the couch, but not quickly, because he wanted to get caught. "And I was too, guessing all those outlandish names."

"And you knew the whole time."

He reached the end of the couch and waited there until his husband crawled between his thighs and pinned him to the cushion. "I did."

"How? When?"

"I found out when we were investigating the Magnolia Queen murders," Sawyer said. "Rocky's aunt let it slip when I interviewed her about our suspect."

"Christ. That was years ago."

Sawyer slid his hand into Royce's hair. "Uh-huh."

"You could've ended my silly game at any point."

"Where would the fun be in that?" Sawyer asked him. "I believe you were going to wipe the dog slobber off your mouth and put it to good use. Something about delivering a big package."

Royce snatched a baby wipe from the packet on the end table, just one of the many they'd conveniently placed everywhere for quick cleanup. Before Darla came into their lives, Royce had stashed lube in every nook and cranny. Oh, how the times had shifted, but Sawyer wouldn't change a thing.

"So industrious." He pulled Royce to him for a hot, hungry kiss that promised a swift delivery.

Darla's cries came through the monitor, and Dolly jumped to her feet, barking at the invisible threat. Royce buried his face in Sawyer's crotch with a groan, and Sawyer carded his fingers through silky blond strands.

"I'll feed the baby while you build the workbench," Sawyer said.

Royce swiped his tongue over Sawyer's neck in the possessive lick that drove him wild. "Next nap, your ass is mine."

"I'm going to hold you to it."

EPILOGUE

Two and a half months later...

"IN MY THIRTY YEARS ON THE BENCH, I'VE NEVER SEEN AN outpouring of love like this one," Judge Hampton said, gesturing to the crowd gathered in the courtroom. "It's extremely touching to be a part of this journey with you."

Royce and Sawyer turned and smiled at their family, friends, and colleagues smooshed together like sardines in the small room. They were loved by the most incredible people, but seeing the outpouring in full display on the most important day of their lives was next-level special.

"It is my absolute honor to confirm that the adoption of Darla Grace Locke is final. Royce Locke and Sawyer Locke are her legal parents from this moment on, with all the associated rights and responsibilities. I wish your family a lifetime of health and happiness, gentlemen." The clerk handed her a piece of paper, which she signed with a flourish. "I've signed the decree and ordered a new birth certificate to be issued for Darla Grace Locke showing both her fathers as her parents." Judge Hampton set the pen down and crossed her hands on the bench. "And that concludes the hearing."

Cheering and clapping broke out in the room, but the judge didn't bang the gavel and call the court to order. She smiled indulgently as Royce and Sawyer teared up.

"Thank you so much, Your Honor," Ivy said once the courtroom quieted. "Would you be willing to pose for a few pictures with Darla and her fathers?"

"It would be my honor." Judge Hampton pushed back from the bench and stepped down. She shook their hands and congratulated them before fussing over Darla. "We can pull your immediate family out of that army to be included in the photos."

Royce waved over the parents and siblings, who immediately enveloped Darla and her dads in hugs. He crooked his finger at Kelsey and Ella. "We need our best girls in here."

"I'll take the photos," Andrew said.

"Baby," Ella said, clapping her hands.

Darla giggled and grinned at Kels and Ella when they stepped up next to them. Andrew took a few moments to get everyone positioned before shooting several photos in rapid succession. Judge Hampton wished them well again before heading into her chambers. The mob of family and friends shuffled out of the courtroom and into the rotunda, but Royce held Sawyer back for a private moment.

"Happy birthday," Royce said.

Sawyer kissed the top of Darla's head. "Best present ever."

"Do you feel different?" Royce asked.

"I have peace of mind now that the law will recognize me as her legal parent, but I've been her daddy since her first breath. That hasn't changed."

Royce kissed him. "And it never will."

Sawyer cupped his neck and held him in place. "I have loved every version of you, from the angry, brokenhearted soul I first met to this beautiful, healed man who shares a life, a love, and a child with me. Every time I think I couldn't possibly love you more, you prove me wrong. But today is the pinnacle. It doesn't get better than this, baby."

Royce's mouth curved into his trademark smirk. "Challenge accepted."

The End!

Staying in touch is easier than ever and prettier too! Would you like to follow me on all the socials, signup for my newsletter, or join my Facebook reader's group? You can do all those things by checking out this handy hub on my website @ www.aimeenicolewalker.com/links

OTHER BOOKS BY
AIMEE NICOLE WALKER

Curl Up and Dye Mysteries
Dyeing to be Loved
Something to Dye For
Dyed and Gone to Heaven
I Do, or Dye Trying
A Dye Hard Holiday
Ride or Dye
Curl Up and Dye Box Set

Road to Blissville Series

Unscripted Love
Someone to Call My Own
Nobody's Prince Charming
This Time Around
Smoke in the Mirror
Inside Out
Prescription for Love

Welcome to Blissville Collection (Both M/M Blissville series)
Volume One
Volume Two

The Lady is Mine Series
The Lady is a Thief
The Lady Stole My Heart

Queen City Rogue Series
Broken Halos
Wicked Games
Beautiful Trauma

Zero Hour Series
Ground Zero
Devil's Hour
Zero Divergence
Zero Hour Box Set

Sawyer and Royce: Matrimony and Mayhem
The Magnolia Murders
Marriage is Murder
Killer Honeymoon

Sawyer and Royce: Felonies and Fatherhood
The Paternity Puzzle
The Sinner's Son

Sinister in Savannah Series
Ride the Lightning
Mr. Perfect
Pretty Poison
Sinister in Savannah Box Set

Savannah Universe Standalone Books
Invisible Strings
Bad at Love
About Last Night
Just Say When
Single in Savannah Box Set

Standalone Novels
Second Wind

Fated Hearts Series
Chasing Mr. Wright
Rhythm of Us
Surrender Your Heart
Perfect Fit

Redemption Ridge Series
Guys Like Him
The Fortunate Son
Saints Like Him
Friends Like Them
The Keeper
The Beautiful Mess
Starts With a Bang

Coauthored with Nicholas Bella
Undisputed
Circle of Darkness (Genesis Circle, Book 1)
Circle of Trust (Genesis Circle, Book 2)

ACKNOWLEDGMENTS

Many, many thanks to Charity, Sandra, and Lori for your editing services and for keeping me in line. These ladies are consummate professionals and are pure joy to work with. And much love to Natasha Snow for this gorgeous cover and to Stacey Ryan Blake for her stunning interior designs. All of you make my books sparkle and shine so beautifully—inside and out. I thank my lucky stars that I get to work with such wonderfully talented people.

Sending much love to Melinda James Rueter and Racheal Yunk for bravely reading my rough drafts and providing priceless feedback. And I don't know where I'd be without CC Belle, my amazing personal assistant, who brings organization and so much joy into my life. Love you, ladies!

xoxo
Aimee

ABOUT
AIMEE NICOLE WALKER

Aimee Nicole Walker is an international bestselling author of Male/ Male contemporary romance and romantic suspense novels. Her stories guarantee hunks with big…hearts, lots of humor and heat, and the occasional homicide. Aimee is a lifelong dreamer, an avid reader, and an off-key singer. Only two of those traits help her craft captivating characters and charming communities where everyone is welcome. She uses the other quirk to entertain her pets during writing breaks.

Aimee has loved the same guy for over thirty years. Her husband is the reason she can write romance novels, and he's possibly inspired a fictional murder plot a time or ten. They share three adult children, two adorable grandsons, and a menagerie of pets that don't include goats or donkeys…yet. Love inspires everything she does, books keep her sane, and coffee is the magic elixir that fuels her day.

Let's stay in touch!

Would you like to learn more about my work, sign up for my newsletter, or follow my social media accounts? Here's your fast pass to all things Aimee:

www.ingramcontent.com/pod-product-compliance
Lightning Source LLC
Chambersburg PA
CBHW031424250626
47155CB00004B/1617